KING'S CATCH

SENTINEL SECURITY NYC
BOOK 1

ELIZA RENTON

KING'S CATCH

SENTINEL SECURITY NYC
FIRST IN SERIES

Maggie witnessed the murder of her brother and best friend. New York City was her escape plan, except now she's sleeping on the streets, with a dollar to her name. Luckily, Sentinel Security just hired her as a translator.

Winter is ex-Delta Force, an elite sniper, now part of Sentinel's NYC operation. A loner. Winter is not looking for a roommate. Definitely not a woman as sweetly packaged as Sentinel's new interpreter. Trouble with a capital T.

When Maggie's dangerous past lands on Winter's doorstep, he vows to protect her. But can she trust him to keep her safe, or will her heart keep on running?

King's Catch contains sex scenes between mutually consenting adults. Open the door and off with the clothes. Winter cusses, swears sometimes, but never at Maggie.

ACKNOWLEDGMENTS

Where would I be without the most patient of editors - Jody Wallace (Mean Kitty Editing). Any errors you find in this book are all down to me.

Eagle eye, Louise, never tires of my anxious requests to read early drafts of my stories. I am in her debt.

As always, my writing group, The Saturday Ladies Bridge Club, offers ongoing support. Thank you, ladies.

And to the wonderful women in my knitting group. You keep me sane!

For Gary. My soul mate who left this earth much too soon. Often in my thoughts. Fond memories of living and dancing in downtown Manhattan.

PROLOGUE

LOSING the will to live in Afghanistan. The same damn place Winter had been for his last two tours and now a third, thank Christ, final tour. This stuff was getting old.

He had no problem with how he'd got to spend his summer in the mountains of the Hindu Kush—9/11 made the world stand up and take notice. Within a week, he had been at the front of the recruitment line, heels clicking together, right hand over his heart. More than eager to sign the papers. But it was time already. Move on, get a life that didn't involve living off MREs. Swap his weapon for a fishing rod.

"So, what you got planned, Winter?" Lewis asked.

With a snort, Winter glared at his best friend.

"What? You know. After?" Lewis scraped his hand through his carrot mop and winked.

Ever since they were hand-picked and transferred from the Rangers to Delta Force, the man had been his best friend. Winter shook his head. "Haven't got a clue, Smiley."

No prizes for guessing how he got his code name. Holed

up in the middle of nowhere, surrounded by dirt and rocks with the sun and flies competing for who'd be the first to eat them alive, this cock-eyed optimist beamed the same face-ache grin he'd sported every day since Winter had known him.

"Don't be shy, Winter. Life's no fun without a plan. Take me. Once I'm on home turf, I going to barbecue me a bigger-than-Christmas rib-eye while I knock back a very long, cold beer. Next, I'll ask a willing woman to... Now, I think on it. Not necessarily in that order."

"Yeah, yeah. I get the fucking picture."

"So?" Smiley insisted.

"Fishing in the Bahamas." Didn't hurt to ditch his shit attitude and dream. Except the deep ache in his bones warned him to stay alert. Not to let his down his guard.

Dressed in full camouflage, he and Smiley perched on the hilltop, assault rifles aimed at Achmed Hassad's latest hide-out. Surrounded by at least a dozen armed guards, the terrorist compound stuck out like a single hair on a bald man's head.

If today turned out to be a good day, he expected the murdering psychopath to exit soon for his latest cameo performance. A beheading. Only one thing turned Hassad on more than decapitating anyone who looked sideways at him, and that was filming the shit for his fans. Since daybreak, the latest in a line of sorry fucks had been hanging by his wrists in the clearing. Begging for his life.

"How much do you reckon one of those new F-150 SVT Raptor Super Cab pickups will set me back?" Smiley nudged his elbow.

That's where Lewis spent time in his head, hanging out

in a New Jersey car yard, imagining his ass parked in Ford's latest truck. "Forty-five thou, give or take a nickel or two." Winter checked his weapon.

"No problem. I got that. Yeah."

Smiley half-raised a fist, no doubt picturing the pot of gold in his locker. Winter aspired to nothing that lofty. Off base. Home in Brooklyn, talking shit on the stoop with his neighbors. A week with a barrel of his favorite whiskey suited fine. Last week's letter from Senora Ortega, full of how hell-hot summer in New York had been this year, didn't faze him, even if the humidity kept on climbing.

Every month she sent him an email catching him up on the hood. Might not realize how her neighborly intel kept him from losing his mind. Same went for her chocolate chip cookie care package.

Except there wasn't much left of his appetite or his soul. Between tours he'd visited home, a dead man walking through Brooklyn, unable to see much beyond the horror of all he had done in his country's name.

"Shit." Winter swore as a vicious cramp chewed into his calf. Twenty-four hours, going on an eternity, their asses had kissed the dust under the camouflage netting, unable to take a full breath in case they were spotted. Any sudden move, like hopping around on one leg on a fucking mountain top, could get his head blown off.

"Vehicles approaching at three o'clock," Smiley warned.

"Yeah, I see them." Fucking surprise visitors. The worst kind. From day one, nothing related to this mission had gone right. The plan had been a quick in and out. Shoot the asshole enemy and return to base. Instead, Hassad hadn't so much as poked a finger outside his quarters, let alone his head. Either he had a severe case of the squirts or one hell of a passionate woman keeping him in bed.

Winter watched as the vehicle approached the compound. The guard tormenting the strung-up prisoner stuck his boot into his victim one last time before running toward it. Adrenaline percolated under Winter's Kevlar. As a warm-up, he should shoot the fucker.

Below them, the rest of his team were on the move, preparing to roll out the welcome mat. Winter focussed on the entrance to Hassad's hut. *Come to daddy, dickwad.* Show me the tip of your goddam nose. One kill shot before he and Smiley joined Cookie and Robot and made their exit.

"Oh yeah. Who said dreams don't come true?" Smiley whispered.

Winter chuckled.

Larger than life, Hassad lurched into the daylight and yelled at the driver of the truck.

Winter exhaled, consciously slowed his heart rate, and squeezed the trigger. Easy as pissing. Hassad's brains splattered over the idiot standing too close to his leader. On his next breath, he searched through the scope of his HK417 for the driver and found him crumpled beside the truck. *Shit, yeah.* Trust Smiley to treat him to the same mind-blowing day as Hassad.

"Target down. Mission accomplished. Over," Winter confirmed over the comms, the words rolling over his tongue, smooth as a single malt. Preparing to move out, he packed his gear. Meanwhile, the compound had erupted. Too late, people swarmed out of their huts, panic rising, before shit blew sideways.

Smiley was ahead, sliding over the hill toward Robot and

Cookie. Far from dead, Hassad's driver sprang to his feet. Faster than light, he flipped open the canvas, reached into the back of his truck, and dragged out an RPG.

Focused on the chaos immediately in front of him, Smiley hadn't seen the driver's miraculous rise from the fucking dead. "Down. Get the hell down," Winter bellowed. One hand steadying his descent, rocks rolling under his feet, he scrambled to stay upright and reach his teammate.

Too late. A deafening roar and a mushroom cloud of grey smoke shrouded the spot where he'd last seen him.

"Robot, Cookie, anybody, talk to me." Winter pressed his earpiece and kept running. None of them answered. Later, he'd swear he saw his best bud zip past him, one hand on the wheel of a spanking new pickup, the other raised in a one-finger salute. Smiley's face ingrained in Winter's mind forever.

CHAPTER
ONE

FIVE LONG YEARS alive when he should be long dead. Winter shook the rain from his cap, scraped a hand through his hair and fixed his cap tight on his head. As he gave his fishing pole a shake, he thought of Senora Ortega. It must bore her god stupid, the one she prayed to, lit candles for every Sunday, watching his sorry ass relive that sorry day.

Suck it up. No medals handed out for wallowing in service shit. After being honorably discharged from the armed forces, he'd worked for several security firms before joining Sentinel last year. Everyone on his new team lived with stuff they never spoke about to anyone.

No judgement. Snake, the boss understood, gave them forty-eight hours to flip the cell to silent and chill, but God help the guy who didn't turn up to the office ready to roll on day three.

Like him, they had their own back after-mission ritual. Trigger hit the bars. Fucked the brains out of any willing partner. Storm pulled the sheet over his head and refused to acknowledge daylight. Mowgli sat in front of the TV and ordered takeout. Havoc, who was as good as married to Mia, never shared. His shit-eating grin said it all. Lucky fuck.

Day two and Winter sat at the end of the Valentino Pier taking in the view over the East River. After military service, he had gone home to Brooklyn. The place where he grew up. The familiar sounds and smells of Red Hook beat at the same pace as his heart.

Through the mist, Lady Liberty stood proud. A little further, the Manhattan skyline towered beyond Governor's Island, the peaks of buildings disappearing into the low clouds.

As soon as they landed in the country, Snake, regular as clockwork, pulled him aside, asked if he was doing okay. Did he need anything? Nope, he was fine. His answer never changed. Hanging out here, he didn't have to pretend. He coped with the fact that every time he woke up, a part of him questioned why fate had spared him and not blown him to dust with his friends. His brothers.

Winter propped his fishing rod against the railing and sighed. Perhaps he'd take Trigger up on his offer and join him later at Joe Joe's. A downtown mecca for the lonely.

The rain had eased enough to hear the ripple of water hitting the small rocks leading from the shoreline into the water. With only the fish for company, striped bass if he was lucky, he could spit, swear, bawl his fucking eyes out without witnesses.

No one to pat his shoulder, or worse, give him a smile, laced with a concern he didn't deserve or appreciate. These days, Senora Ortega's chocolate chip cookies were the only comfort he required. Lately, she'd taken to adding macadamias, refusing to listen when he insisted not even her sweet baking could make him less bitter.

Overhead, clouds came and went, tossed along by the wind. At the other end of the pier, flags clanged against the poles, and the few people who'd ventured out to take the dog for a walk chatted amongst themselves.

Winter peered over the rail at the gray water. The swell might scare away any fish, but he baited his line and tossed it over the side. After being cooped up in the plane home for fourteen hours, it felt good to be outside. He couldn't get much wetter, so why not lean back, stretch his legs, and enjoy the icy wind biting his cheeks?

Hell, he was tired. He turned the bill of his cap face-forward to protect his sunglasses. All part of the charade. People thought twice about bugging a man wearing shades in the rain. Winter by name, but he still hungered for that sunny beach in the Bahamas.

Freezing his ass off, he lured fish, who, thanks to New York's catch and release laws, would spend less than two minutes swinging from his hook. Fucking tragic.

Bracing one foot on the railing, he kept his eye on his rod and retrieved the flask of hot coffee from his bag. These days, he didn't drink much alcohol, the odd beer, an occasional whiskey, but he never said no to good coffee. Single origin, strong and dark.

Shit that never quit bothering him circled around in his head. The loneliness. It wasn't a place he went to very often, but he had a strong suspicion if Sentinel hadn't offered him that job a year ago, he would have thrown it in for good. They valued his skill set, courtesy of a government that had invested millions in his killing education.

On this last mission, they had rescued a senator's daughter and taken her home from Venezuela. Not pretty. Gentlemen didn't kidnap teenagers and hold them for ransom. Calling them pigs was an insult to the animal.

Evil shit, money. And thanks to his granddad's obsession with the greenback, he had inherited more than he needed. First thing he did when he got home was to buy the brownstone he lived in, equip it with the latest high-tech systems, and furnish it how he liked it. He'd given thousands to people who could genuinely use the stuff. Fucking tough, what some had to deal with. The gesture burned the interest on his savings accounts. Nothing more.

Try harder.

Thank God, he didn't intend living a second past fifty. With ten years to go, the sooner he made it to that beach in the Bahamas, the better.

Winter's gaze drifted to the couple who sat on the bench a few yards to his right, their lover's argument playing havoc with his day. Hadn't they noticed the man with a rod trying to catch a damn fish?

The woman, a good-looking blond, had arrived first. Alone, glancing over her shoulder. Nervous. Hard to miss wearing her emerald-green beanie. When the rain started, she took it off, which made no sense, and rolled her curls into a knot on top of her head. A popular style, but why be careless with the asset?

Coz, she's not out to please you, asshat. Sam's voice rang in his ear. The boss' wife considered it her personal mission to keep their chauvinistic shit in line.

Slowly, the blond had walked to the end of the pier, her slim hips swaying to the syncopated rhythm of the universe.

He'd read that last bit in a poem when he was at school, and it stuck. Mainly because Mandy Philips, the hottest girl in junior high, with her blacker than black pigtails and green eyes, had been his first crush. Scribbling her note with the poem had impressed. Nothing stirred his arousal like watching a woman walk. The sexy swing of a firm, round ass.

Goddam, if this pair failed to shut the hell up in the next ten seconds, he just might make that call to Trig, even if it took more energy than he cared to use, convincing a woman you just met at Joe Joe's you were more than the drinks you kept on coming, that you appreciated conversation and getting laid could wait. Yeah, he wasn't sure he believed it either.

Shit, this guy had a low-life mouth. Without turning, Winter pushed his sunglasses further onto the bridge of his nose and coughed. Normally, he might choose to mind his own business, but there was something about the blond that piqued his interest. Eyes front, he kept her in his peripheral vision, in case the skinny dude made a move to match his mouth.

Not acceptable. Their escalating garbage, combined with the rain drumming on the pier, was scaring the damn fish and playing havoc with Winter's day.

CHAPTER
TWO

WINTER LOWERED his shades to the tip of his nose. He didn't have to guess why they were arguing. The woman's body language expressed it all. *She ain't into you, dude, and if you grab her again, stuff will get ugly.* He half hoped the skinny guy did. He would enjoy teaching Doofus that no meant no.

That said, their bullshit was seriously grating, and he had an early start at Sentinel tomorrow. A last nod to Lady Liberty, disappearing into an ominous cloud before he hightailed it for home. His fridge was empty. On the way back he'd make a stop at Trader Joe's, and stock up before the weekend.

"Come on, Mags. This is insane. I'm freezing. We stay here much longer and we'll both catch pneumonia." Douche reached for her arm.

Guess he wasn't leaving soon. Winter propped his rod against the railing and stepped forward.

"Let go of me. And don't call me Mags! I told you I've found somewhere else to live. Closer to work."

Okay. I could have been hasty. Blondie was coping, so he

shifted his weight and shoved his flask and tackle into his bag.

"Work? You got a job? When? That's great. On the way home we'll stop at a cash machine, and you can pay me the week's rent you owe," the guy said with a sneer.

"I don't owe you anything, Kenny. You never gave me your share of the grocery money or the fifty bucks I lent you last week." She dragged her beanie from her pocket and pulled it over her head. "We'll call it even. Now leave me alone."

Winter took his time sorting his hooks. Along with cleaning them, something he usually waited to do when he got home. *Damn.* He could have sworn he crimped the hook enough to flatten off the barb. Blood spotted the end of his finger. *Yeah. Not his fucking day.*

Mags was doing a good job standing up to Kenny, but his gut said, stay, so he didn't plan on leaving yet. Knowing better than to mess with his instincts, he grabbed a clean scrap and pressed it over the scratch.

This time when douche snared her arm, she cried out and stumbled when she dragged herself away. Before shit-for-brains could scramble together his next sentence, Winter had Kenny's shirt wrapped in his fist and was close enough to steam up his glasses.

"Look, dude, I don't want to interrupt." *Like fuck, he didn't.* Easing back, he gestured to the blond. "But do as the lady asks and move along? You're scaring her and the fish." He added a meaningful poke to asshat's chest.

Mags tugged on her ear. "I'm sorry. We're leaving. Aren't we, Kenny?"

"Nah, changed my mind. Free country. I like it here." Kenny folded his arms and flopped onto the wet bench.

This idiot had a death wish. At six and a half feet, Winter towered over the two. He guessed Mags must be five-five, slim, thin-boned. Looked fourteen but had to be in her twenties. Young. Too fucking young to be facing off with this jerk, and when her gaze latched onto her shoes, he wanted to apologize. Scaring her made him no better than the other guy.

"Why don't you mind your own damn business and get back to your fish, old man," Kenny muttered and snatched the woman's arm.

Fucking rude calling people names. He may be ten years older, but he had a very short fuse. Smacking this moron into the middle of next week would perk up his shitty day. "Plan to, Junior, as soon as you let go of your girlfriend's arm. I may be old, but I'm not deaf, and she told you to leave her alone." He raised his chin in Mags' direction. "Time to go. Right?"

"Er… sorry. Yes, night time comes around quickly this time of year. Do you fish here often?" With more power than he expected, she shook herself free of Kenny, tugged her damn ear again.

Winter shook his head. Not the answer he'd expected, and he regretted getting involved. No obvious signs, but the two of them could be high as kites. Time to bail and leave the lovebirds to kiss and make up.

Suddenly, Junior sprang forward. Winter widened his stance, prepared to take him on, but Kenny pushed past and stomped off along the pier. The blond didn't stop him. Simply stared into the damp mist swirling over the East

River and brushed her cheek with the sleeve of her sweater.

Seeing a woman cry always made for a challenge. His arm had a mind of its own, itching to swing around their shoulders while he did his best to make them stop. "Hey, he's gone. You need a ride home?" Winter ordered his arm to stay put by his side. He didn't have a clue where she lived, but he had parked his truck a block over.

She shook her head. No problem. By the time he finished packing, she hadn't moved from the spot where he'd left her, staring out over the water.

"Seriously, are you okay?" He shuffled his feet to let her know he was still there and waited for her to tell him to get lost, too.

"Run away? I thought about it, but I'm tired."

"Huh?" Winter scratched his head. He was in no mood for weird word games, and if she kept tugging on her ear, it would fall off. A tiny, delicate ear perfect for the tip of his tongue. Her gaze ducked, not for the ground this time, but for his lips. The visual caress of his mouth made his cock twitch. "You sure you're okay?" he repeated.

"Yes, thank you. But you're bleeding. Her eyes fixed on his mouth as she pointed to his hand.

"It's minor. I'll fix it when I get home."

"No need. I have a Band-Aid."

Winter raised his eyebrow.

"I know. Crazy. I have the pockets of a twelve-year-old. Stuffed with tissues, candy, a couple of dollars. Lucky for you, I thought of everything. Ah, here it is. One Band-Aid."

His mouth gaped open and shut. *Who the hell was this woman?*

"Come on. Give me your hand. I hope you don't faint at the sight of blood." She laughed.

Winter shook his head while his heart levitated. Yep, like an air balloon on a windy day. "Thanks, but I'll survive without the Band-Aid." If she could see the size of the holes in his body, she'd understand. Not that there was a chance of that happening.

"You don't want to get an infection. They can be very nasty. People with cuts a lot less scary than this die from blood poisoning. You need to take care of it. Give me your hand." Palm facing up, she waited. "It's my favorite, Mini Mouse. Rare. There's always twice as many Mickeys in a box." She wiggled the Disney dressing in front of him and winked.

Fair enough. Winter did as she asked. As she secured the Band-Aid, electric shocks shot from her fingertips straight to his cock. The most awake it had been in a long time.

And, with no warning, Maggie brushed her lips against her finished job. "There, a kiss to make it better."

What was he, five? "I will give you a ride home," he choked.

"Thank you, but no need. I don't live far."

"No trouble. I'm parked two minutes away on Ferris."

"Thanks, but..."

"'Fraid I won't take no for an answer. Not in this lousy weather." The rain had set in for the night. "It's getting dark. Besides, I might bleed to death." Holding up his hand, he wiggled his fingers and smiled. Something else he rarely did.

"Can't have that, can we?" she said, adding a wide, honest smile that defied anyone to deny its generosity before she shivered.

Winter took off his jacket and tossed it over her shoulders. Didn't like it much when she cringed, and a stray curl escaped from her beanie and fell on her neck. He almost dived in for a taste, a smell of what he knew would be sweet.

Instead, he directed his boots past the flagpole to where he'd parked his ride, shortening his stride so Mags didn't have to struggle to keep up with him. She hesitated at Hoek's, the pizza place on the corner. Back on the pier, her stomach had growled. Hungry? She certainly looked as though she could do with some carbs.

"Mind if I stop for a second? I need to use the bathroom," she said, before he could ask her to join him for dinner.

"No problem. Do you want to…"

"Look. Sorry, I didn't catch your name."

"Winter."

"Well, Winter, it's good of you to offer me a ride, but I can walk from here."

Interesting. In a blink, she had gone from kissing his hand to shoving away. Too bad he wasn't ready to ditch her in the back streets of Red Hook this late at night. Soaked to the skin. "Do what you have to—I'll wait."

"Oh, okay," she said and disappeared inside the restaurant.

And wait, he did for all of ten minutes. Long enough for anyone to do what they had to do in the washroom. Earlier, he'd noticed her crying. What if the Kenny shit had hit her harder than he suspected? He stepped inside Hoek. Local, so he knew the place well. The restrooms were in the back. Serving a couple, he spotted Jenny, one of the regular waitresses. He waited until she'd finished and asked, "Hey Jen, do me a favor."

"Winter. Twice in a week. Unusual for you. Here for your usual?"

"Nah, thanks. Not here to eat. A friend. Er, she wasn't feeling too great. Went to the restroom. Could you check? See if she's okay, for me?"

"Sure, hang on."

Two minutes passed before she reappeared, shaking her head. "There's no one there. Looks like your chicken has flown the coop. Sorry." She wiped her hands on her apron and turned to the table next to her. "What can I get you?"

CHAPTER
THREE

UGH. Soaked to the skin, Maggie's body trembled. She loved rain, but knowing she had to sleep outside tonight, she wished it would stop for a few hours. As well as his body heat, Winter's musky scent permeated the leather jacket hanging over her shoulders. She pulled the edges together under her chin and willed herself to quit shivering.

Public restrooms were a major trigger. Five years and a thousand visits to shrinks, but the memory of Steve and Josie, her best friend's murders, never faded. Never would.

She'd hang on for hours to avoid using one, but she figured Winter wouldn't follow her there. Kenny owned that kind of psycho. He would have, for sure. Take today, turning up at the pier. How many times did a girl have to tell a dude it was over?

Under her damp clothes, she was sweating, because the guy, insisting he give her a ride home, might have spooked him, but Kenny was a gigantic brick wall when it came to getting what he wanted.

Odd, now she thought about it, despite Winter's size—

massive, a tower of solid muscle—he didn't scare her like Kenny did. The cowboy boots poking from under the cuff of his faded jeans suited him in a retro Sheriff Woody way, and the flecks of gray speckled through the stubble on his chin added to his reliable vibe. His lips were full. Sensuous. Score heaven for his eyes. Sharp, black beacons gleaming with intelligence that missed nothing.

Turning on the tap, she ran her ice-cold fingers under the hot water faucet. She could kick herself for staying so long at Kenny's but finding work in a new city had proved a lot harder than expected. Every morning she woke up telling herself the perfect job was only her next interview away.

A friend of her brother's—how that happened she would never know—Kenny had offered her a place to stay when she left Boston. Leaving her job at the university had not been easy. She loved her work, but after the fire in the stair-well of her apartment complex, she'd been too scared to live alone.

The police figured it had been a warning to residents not to snitch on neighborhood drug dealers. When they made it clear they had more serious crimes to investigate, there wasn't much point in telling them about the heavy breather bugging her.

It wasn't the first time she had moved on. After Lazenby murdered her brother and friend, his family had harassed her, swore they would follow through on the threats he'd made from jail. After so long, she couldn't be sure what had triggered them now, but figured they were stalking her again.

A couple of nights ago, Kenny had headed out to his dealer. He scored every night. Buried under the thin blanket in his freezing cold apartment, she had tried to sleep, to stay clear of her nightmares and not hear the man shouting. See him raise his gun and shoot Steve and Josie.

Finally, she'd nodded off, only to wake up and find Kenny lying next to her in bed. Psycho. Technically, it was his bed, but they had a deal. He slept on the sofa, and no funny business. His excuse. *I enjoy watching you sleep, listening to you snore.* What the hell. Angry, terrified. It took five minutes to pack her travel bag and get the hell out of there.

Maggie shuddered. She had a job interview tomorrow. Fingers crossed, twirl three times and toss in a Hail Mary for good luck, the company would hire her because sleeping on the streets was not in the least bit romantic. Every rustle, animal screech and thunder roll scared the crap out of her. If she got the job, she'd ask for an advance and find somewhere to live.

Maggie stuck her head out into the narrow corridor of the pizza place. A guy in a chef's top, chopping onions with the speed of a ninja, standing behind the serving hatch in the wall opposite, hadn't noticed her.

Before she opened the rear exit, she listened for any sound on the other side of the metal door. In her hurry to leave Kenny's, she had left her hearing aid. Too much to expect that the reason he'd shown up today was to do her a favor and return it.

She tugged on her ear. Straining to hear gave her a headache, which nine times out of ten turned into a raging migraine. Her fault Kenny had found her because she'd made the mistake of mentioning how the view from the pier calmed her.

Maggie pushed open the door and stepped into the dimly lit street. After checking in the direction where she last saw Winter, she hurried along the narrow sidewalk and slipped behind the wire fence into the school and retrieved her bag. She'd hidden it in the garden shed, a couple of blocks from the park where she'd been sleeping.

Maggie pulled the beanie over her ears. Knitting it had used up all her yarn, which was a pain. Not being able to knit, watch her needles working, made her extra nervous. Winter's coat felt amazingly warm. It swamped her arms and body and almost reached her knees, but the damp musky smell spiked with lime reminded her of how gentle his touch had been when he laid it on her shoulders.

Could there be a way to return it? *'Fraid not. Maggie King, Coat Thief.* If reincarnation was a thing, she was doomed to come back as a cockroach.

She rolled her lips together. If she wanted to have the subway fare to travel to Manhattan tomorrow, she'd need to skip dinner. Swallowing that less than happy thought, she stepped off the sidewalk.

"Lady, watch where you're going. You wanna get yourself killed?" a guy yelled as he whizzed past on his e-scooter.

"Sorry." Smiling nervously, she dashed to the sidewalk. No, she wasn't trying to get dead. She simply hadn't heard him, but if she wanted a job, she needed to arrive for the interview in one piece. Damned if she knew where he'd come from. She shook her head. Except for a parked bike and a car, the street was empty.

The small park she had slept in was as good as any place the past few nights, but with the rain not looking as though it would stop anytime soon, she wasn't so sure. Ahead, the kid's playground, with its brightly colored swings and roundabout, slowly spinning in the wind, were eerie, but the smell of rain mixed with the earthy goodness of the plants and trees reminded her of the herbs and small ferns she had kept alive on the balcony in Boston.

Smells often made her feel safe. Fortunately, her nose compensated for not hearing stuff well. Maggie was the first to smell the fire in the stairwell and had warned everyone to leave before anyone got hurt.

Not wanting to think of the squirrels and whatever other rodents ran around after dark, she had scoped out a spot at one end of the park. Aside from a few clothes, she didn't have much except an old pair of sweatpants and a shirt to make a bed.

One of the garbage bags she'd picked up at the local store, spread as evenly as possible over the wet ground, covered with a pair of old sweatpants, made a half-decent mattress. A folded top became a pillow. A second plastic bag, snagged on a tree branch above her head, would shelter her body from some of the rain.

Oh, no, Maggie King. You do not get to cry. Several times since she left the restaurant, she had pushed aside the temptation to run to Kenny's.

Arms folded, she stared at the makeshift bedroom and filled her head with thoughts of sunshine. This could work. In the morning, she could wash up in the restroom at Penn Station. It was time to bed down for the night when her cell rang. Quickly, she fished it out of her bag.

"Hello. Who's this?" she asked, mildly panicked that Kenny had found her.

"Maggie King?" A deep voice answered.

23

"Yes. What do you want?" She switched the phone to her good side so she could hear better.

"It's Detective Esposito, Ms King. Where are you?"

A chill ran through the hairs on the back of her neck. She recognised his voice but hadn't heard from the detective since they had convicted Lazenby five years ago. "Brooklyn. New York. Why?" she asked, dreading his answer.

"Good. That's good. My chief said you might be here in Boston."

"No. Why are you calling?" Her voice trembled.

"Nothing to be alarmed about, but we thought you should know that Rick Lazenby escaped from prison."

Her knees buckled. Maggie reached for the fence and slowly sank onto her bed. "When?" she squeaked.

"Three weeks ago," the detective answered, obviously embarrassed.

"Why didn't you tell me before?" Ever since she'd been the prime witness for the prosecution and Lazenby had promised to kill her first chance he got, the lawyers and police had agreed she would be the first to know if there were any changes in his circumstances.

"I apologize. A mix up with the paperwork. Lazenby would be a fool to come after you, but keep your eyes open, Ms. King. Report anything unusual. Where did you say you were living?"

"Er, New York." She worried her lip with her tongue. Should she have told him? Was it better to disappear and hope no one found her?

"If you give me your address, I can let NYPD know what's happening and they'll keep an eye out. I'll request they send an officer round to check on you."

She wanted to believe that was true, but honestly? Stretched to the max, they weren't likely to spend any time babysitting her. "I'm between places right now. When I have my new address, I will forward it to you. Thanks for calling."

"Like I said. Sorry, it took so long. Take care Ms. King. Have a good evening."

She swallowed the lump in her throat and sighed. "Thank you. Same to you." Tears streamed over her cheeks. Pulling her feet under the cover of the makeshift shelter, she tucked into a ball and did her best to sob silently.

CHAPTER
FOUR

"GO HASSLE SOMEONE ELSE." Winter jerked his knee, expecting George to move his ass and give him space. No such luck. The springer spaniel, Sentinel's three-legged K9, had designated him entertainment for the day and there was no shifting the mutt's butt.

"That dog sure has the hots for you," Storm said, stifling a yawn.

His fellow Bravo team member sat next to him in Sentinel's briefing room. Legs stretched out front, hands linked behind his head, Storm was more than content to let him take the heavy slobber load. Along with Alpha team, they'd been waiting twenty minutes for Snake, the boss, to show and start the meeting.

Not a great start. If Winter believed in bad omens, he might take Snake being late as a sure sign they were in for some shit luck.

"Yeah. Beats me. Trig's the one who loves dogs." Winter raised his chin at his teammate, who was grabbing coffee and chatting to Linda, their new receptionist.

Storm followed his gaze but didn't comment. He would. Just a matter of time before his curiosity got the better of him. Linda, the leggy brunette was a knockout. They were all thankful the boss had hired her. When it came to strategizing, Snake had no equal. Too bad he was shit at paperwork. The latest recruit was an answer to everyone's prayers, so Winter had invited her to dinner, a friendly welcome to the team, surf, and turf at Erics. A trendy uptown, east side bar.

The evening hadn't lasted long. Other than growing up in the same neighborhood, they had nothing in common. Conversation had come to a convenient stop during dessert, and he'd given her a ride home. Should have been the end of it, except Linda kept popping up whenever he was alone. Not wanting to have *that* conversation, he'd opted for the coward's way out, avoiding her ever since. Nothing to be proud of. Soon, tomorrow, they would talk.

"I was going to mind my own business, but I gotta ask. How did it go with Linda the other night? You two an item yet?" Storm asked. A sly grin plastered over his face.

"Shut the hell up, man." Winter wasn't in the mood to discuss it.

George raised his head and whined. "You too." The dog fancied himself as team counsellor, his soulful eyes begging Winter to spill the reason for his crap mood. "Not today, bud."

A wide doggie grin spread across his face the second Winter scratched behind his silky ear. As much as he valued his canine opinion, he was still mulling over why the blond's vanishing act pissed him off. Because it had. Mainly, because he had seen it coming. Plus, she had taken off with his favorite jacket. He'd stayed up most of the night worrying, pacing, trying not to put his fist through the wall.

Winter glanced at the giant clock above the door. The damn ticking irritated the shit out of him. Hard to ignore, the way it marked the seconds, set a rhythm that captured his toe-tapping feet. For reasons that only made sense to Sam, Snake's wife, she had rescued the train station relic from a junk shop in the Catskills and had it fixed. Black Roman numerals stood out against the white face, stained yellow with age and tobacco smoke.

George whined again and shoved his wet nose against Winter's hand. "Yeah, boy, I'm with ya. Lose the antique." One tap of his index finger, and his cell gave him accurate time, destination, how much money he had in the bank, and if the sun would shine. Not today. The same icy wind as yesterday drove the rain in a zig-zag path across the-floor-to-ceiling windows of Sentinel's downtown headquarters.

George twitched at the rolling thunder and shifted a touch. Enough for Winter to reclaim his foot.

"Any idea what we're waiting for?" Trigger asked, nudging the tip of Winter's elbow, and offering him and Storm a mug of coffee.

He took a seat on the other side of Winter. Trigger didn't speak until he was on his third caffeine hit for the day. This morning, he looked a mite green round the gills. Zero sleep and at least one bottle of Jack. No wonder he needed coffee.

"How the fuck should I know?" Winter shrugged.

A loud slurp came from the direction of his feet. "George. For fuck's sake. I appreciate the gesture, buddy, but I can clean my own boots." The dog smiled, but today no gooey canine grins would brighten his mood.

Trig grabbed the canine's collar. "What's got you all bent out of shape this morning?"

"Who, me? I couldn't be better. Had a great night diligently reading today's briefing notes. Should have put them down sooner, but I was goddam riveted."

"That's a fucking lie. You need to get laid, old man."

"Fuck off. And less of the old man shit." The dickhead yesterday, and now Trig. Winter slid deeper into his chair and folded his arms before he punched his friend. Like he'd ever make it that close. Superhuman, Trigger's reflexes. He'd earned his call sign. "And since when am I the eldest? Havoc takes those honors."

"Don't pout," Storm chipped in. "Trig didn't mean to hurt your feelings. Anyway, what the hell did you do yesterday? I thought you were in your happy place—fishing."

"None of your goddam business." He caught Storm's fist a millisecond before it contacted his arm. "Keep your hands to yourself unless you want my toe up your…"

Trigger kicked his boot.

"Incoming."

Winter's jaw gaped open, like one of yesterday's nonexistent fish. "Holy smoked salmon!"

"Easy, man." Trigger shook his head and frowned.

"Fuck easy. That woman stole my coat."

What the hell was she doing here? No bright-colored beanie, no samurai knot. He shifted in his seat as a rare shaft of sunlight bounced through the front window and pinged off the thick braid draped over one shoulder. A few wild strands had escaped and curled like a wave along her long, slim neck, down over her sweater. The forest green number clung to the soft curve of her breasts.

His eyes fixed on her face. *Oh, yeah.* She'd seen him. Sitting two rows from the front, his six foot plus body was fucking hard to miss. Funny, bug eyes on anyone else would have been creepy. On her they looked great. Despite her shock, they shone bright with the same honesty as yesterday, except for smudges of gun-metal gray underneath them. The strained half-smile. She looked done-in exhausted, and that worried him, but he didn't want to freak her out more, so he dropped his gaze to his feet.

Snake took point at the front of the room, Mags by his side. "Good morning, gentlemen. Apologies for keeping you waiting. I realize you all have stuff to do, and I appreciate your patience."

"Patient. Ha, fucking ha," Storm mumbled out the side of his mouth.

Hell, it wasn't like they had a choice. Winter huffed.

"This won't take long," Snake continued. "We have a lot to get through, but first I want to introduce you to Ms. King."

Why the hell was she at Sentinel? An argument with a boyfriend rarely warranted their brand of protection. Or did it? Unease rumbled in his stomach until it lurched for his sternum. Eager for Snake to clarify, Winter leaned forward.

"As of ten minutes ago, Ms. King is the latest member to join Sentinel."

What the fuck?

"Our interview took longer than expected, mainly because, although she came highly recommended, I was unaware of the depth of her skills and the significant contribution she will bring to our organisation."

"Glad to see the boss is all over this one. Our newest

30

recruit is a very attractive addition to Sentinel. Hey Winter, plan on taking her to dinner?" Storm mumbled under his breath.

"Pull your head in dick for brains." He tried to keep his voice low, but Snake looked straight at him and paused. "Sorry boss," he mouthed, feeling ten years old. Sometimes he swore Storm said shit because he needed to hear his own voice.

"Have a seat, Ms. King, and we'll get started." Snake continued. When she hesitated, the boss took her arm and led her to the chair on his right.

Her eyes stayed fixed on the boss the whole time he spoke. Winter knew, because he couldn't stop looking at her. *Yep, definitely paler than yesterday.*

Snake delivered the latest sitrep. Final details would come when they received further intel closer to their departure in the morning. Since he hadn't been joking when he said he'd read the briefing notes, most of the info was nothing new. That fact left headspace to wonder where Maggie kept her woolly beanie. Probably in the pocket of his damn jacket.

"That's all for now, gentlemen. Back here at 0800 tomorrow. Winter, before you go. My office." Snake said, interrupting his wardrobe checklist.

"Oooh, spesh." Storm grinned. Trigger grunted.

"Another word from either of you two dickheads and I swear someone will lose teeth." They enjoyed riling each other. Part of the banter that kept shit light. Most days, Winter didn't bite.

CHAPTER
FIVE

HOLY CRAP! Maggie froze. Of all the people she'd expected to see today, the giant with the sore finger was not one of them. Shocked as she most definitely was, she couldn't resist a smile at the Band-Aid still wrapped around his pinky.

The big kid scowled and rose out of his chair, stalking toward them, black eyes scanning every inch of her. His less than pleased to see her gaze pierced her thumping heart. Probably wondering if she had her eye on another piece of his clothing, which wasn't a bad guess since Maggie would be lying if she said the idea of removing Winter's shirt to sneak a peek at his six-pack hadn't crossed her mind.

Neither of her previous boyfriends had worked out, more nerdy than sporty, but from what she'd seen of her soon-to-be colleagues at Sentinel, all the guys hit the gym at least once a day and ate raw meat for breakfast.

Cool it, Maggie. Technically, she had stolen his coat, an expensive leather jacket.

Snake led the way down the short corridor to another

large room and opened the door with his name on it. "Come in, both of you. This won't take long."

"After you." The tips of Winter's fingers grazed her lower back, sending a shiver dancing up her spine as he showed her to a seat by the window.

The worst place to sit. Too close to traffic noise. First time she met anyone, she felt awkward, stressed, and put off telling them about her disability. Inevitably, they took it as their cue to yell, which never made it any easier to hear them. Of course, she had told Snake. As her new boss, for safety reasons, he had to know. It was the right thing to do. He'd been more than fair, insisting he'd leave it to her how she handled telling everyone else.

Switching direction, she settled into the chair on Winter's right. Most of the time, men spoke fluent chin lifts and single nods. Not exactly a challenge for her lip-reading skills, but sitting there she had a better chance of hearing without having to ask them to repeat anything.

"What do you need, boss?"

"After our chat, I'd like you to show Ms King around HQ. Find her a place to set-up and fill her in on how we operate. Take her to lunch on me. Make her feel welcome. She hasn't been living here very long and doesn't know anyone. You're a born and bred New Yorker, so I'm assigning her to your team for this mission."

"Please." Maggie leaned forward. "I can find my own way around, and I would prefer if everyone called me Maggie." She turned to Winter. "You must have a lot to do, and I've already eaten," she lied, hoping her stomach didn't choose that moment to growl.

"It's no trouble," Snake assured her. "I'll let Maggie fill

you in, but you will agree she has specialist skills. Invaluable to our next mission."

Wow. If that black cloud hanging over Winter's head fell, she'd never get out from underneath it. When they finished here, she should apologize for running out on him last night and pray the growly giant left it there. Now that she had a job, she could promise to have his jacket cleaned before she returned it.

Plan in place she dared to look at him. Thank Christ he'd stopped glaring at her, his attention fully focused on the map Snake was scribbling on the whiteboard. Winter had a strong profile, his nose a little crooked. Steve's nose had had the same kink. Broken at school, defending her from the bully who made fun of her frizzy hair. Flecks of silver feathered the sides of Winter's short dark hair. His lips, her favorite part of human anatomy, were full and sensuous. Yesterday, on the pier, she'd imagined how he kissed.

Winter cleared his throat. Christ on a stick. Had he noticed her checking him out? That habitual frown of his made her kinda sad. Dumb stuff caught her that way sometimes. Steve had laughed and called her over-sensitive.

Raising an eyebrow, Winter unfolded one of his enormous arms and pointed his index-finger at the map spread across Snake's desk.

Yes sir, she mouthed, and sent a silent thank you to anyone listening. A job as Sentinel's interpreter paid three times more than her last position at the university back home, and it was thanks to her old professor that she'd gotten the interview. Impressed by her ability to speak and lip read in several languages, Snake had hired her on the spot.

The man they were going to Pakistan to find, Adnan, knew the whereabouts of a group of nurses kidnapped from an outreach program. Unfortunately, Adnan was deaf and didn't understand a word of English. Aside from Snake, no one knew who hired Sentinel to rescue the women and bring them safely home.

Maggie stared at the map, Snake's voice droning on as he clarified her role for Winter, who stroked the stubble on his chin and grunted every time the boss mentioned her name. Nervous he might convince his boss not to let her go along, beads of sweat moistened her top lip. Horrified, she pulled her hands into her lap and tried not to fidget. All the dispensers in the restrooms at Penn Station had run out of soap and her fingernails were black.

Where she'd slept last night had been filthy. And extremely cold. Thank heaven for Winter's coat or she might have frozen to death. A sudden chill rattled her body.

"You cold? Swap seats." Winter vacated his before she could protest. "Move," he ordered. His eyes twinkled before he gave her a gently nudge with his hip.

Shuffling across, Maggie looked at her boss, waiting for him to call Winter on his rude interruption, but he hadn't seemed to notice. Not long after, Snake finished talking, and she relaxed her shoulders. It took effort dealing with all the input, especially without her hearing aid, and only a few hours' sleep. She had a splitting headache.

"Questions?" Snake asked.

Winter cleared his throat. "No offence, Ms. King," he began.

Here it comes. Maggie held her breath, waiting for the bricks to hit her head.

35

"Are we sure this is a good idea? I'm not doubting your skills, Ms. King."

"Maggie, please," she insisted, hoping that being on a first name basis might soften the growly bear.

"Are we sure? About what?" Snake perched on the edge of his desk and crossed one ankle over the other.

"I have no doubt Ms. Ki…, Maggie, has a-rated skills, but I think we'd all agree she has zip combat skills and there's a high chance we will run into, let's say, interference."

Uncomfortable, much? Nobody enjoyed being talked about as though they weren't in the room, and because of her hearing problem, it happened more times than she liked. "I understand your concern." That part was true, but she couldn't lose this job. "However, I…"

Snake rose to his full height and held up his hand. "Winter. Maggie. This is not a subject for discussion. Not here." He glared at Winter, and her heart plummeted to her feet. What did that mean?

"The reward is worth the risk. We are extremely fortunate that Maggie came along when she did. I consider it a gift that she is fluent in the specific sign language needed to get through to Hassad. A bloody miracle. Order stand, Winter. Any more questions?"

"Yes." Relieved, Maggie half-raised her hand. "Sorry, but how much, er, luggage can I bring?" Winter's grumble rolled through the room. An odd question, but they were flying out of America tomorrow and she had nowhere to stash her stuff. The bits and pieces she had brought from Boston, she didn't want to leave at Kenny's. Before her interview, she'd shoved the canvas bag under the empty reception counter.

Without a word, Snake came around his desk and stood

directly in front of her. Arms folded across his chest, he peered at her. *Adios, new job?*

"How much luggage did you have in mind, Ms. King?"

Back to family names. *Yep, don't let the door touch your behind on your way out.* "Oh, not much.

"Mmm."

"But if that's not possible, I could…" Toss a few items in the trash. She didn't want to, but if it meant keeping her job, she'd sacrifice.

"We'll manage." Snake nodded at Winter. "And now the important matters are out of the way." He winked and her heart fluttered.

Not in the same way as when Winter graced her with an odd smile. Snake's smile was more parental.

"Winter, I will see you and Maggie in the morning."

Both grunted and shared a chin lift. Keen to show solidarity, she did the same and wished her eyes hadn't crossed. More than ruined the effect. Winter blinked twice before fixing her with one of those stares, which made her crazy nervous.

"Come on, I'll give you the tour." He pulled back her chair so she could stand.

Her dad used to do that for her mum. Polite, old fashioned, but the gesture warmed the spot in the center of her chest. *Huh.*

"We'll start with assigning you a locker. With all your luggage, it sounds as though you'll be needing it."

"Oh, hilarious," she muttered, and he laughed. Just her luck the guy's hearing was better than average. Maggie felt the deep rumble through her and settle on her toes. "You should do that more often. It's nice."

37

Winter frowned. "Then we'll hit the gym," he continued, but not before she noticed his cheeks turn a mite pink.

"Great." She hoped he didn't plan on a workout. She had to jog to keep up with his long strides. As they rounded the corner, two people came out of an office. A dog she'd seen earlier in the meeting followed the woman in front. Short hair suited her. The other woman teetering behind her wore a tight skirt and heels.

"Hey, Sam, what brings you in from the kennels?" Winter spoke to the one with the pixie cut and stroked along the dog's spine.

"Careful, Winter. You'll have our latest recruit thinking I'm a stray bitch," she said with a chuckle.

The teetering woman beside her giggled. "Hi, Winter. Talking of lost dogs, I haven't seen you all day. I thought we might catch up in the break. Last night I thought of you." Her fingers stroked the soft part of her neck under her chin. "Stayed up making those cookies you like, double the chocolate chips. Sweet."

Maggie gulped.

"Busy," he mumbled. "Didn't mean to offend." He returned his attention to the woman with the dog. "Sorry, Sam. Not used to seeing you slumming it at HQ is all."

Winter's gaze dropped and Maggie shifted quickly, accidentally stomping on his foot as she hurried to stand in front of him. She wasn't sure who these women were, but she didn't appreciate the way they embarrassed him.

"Hi, I'm Sam." The short-haired woman offered her hand.

Tentatively, Maggie shook it. "Pleased to meet you, I'm Maggie."

"Don't worry about Winter." Sam smiled. "He can take care of himself. I'm married to Snake and the K9 handler for the team. My furry friend here is Bounce, and we're hunting for her three-legged mate, George. This is Linda. She's new too. Hired to save my husband's administrative neck. Snake tells me you have off-the-chart interpreting skills. Finally, great to see him hiring more women. Usually, I stay home. Far too much testosterone kicking around here. But now, I reckon I'll be visiting more often."

The look in Sam's eyes was as steady as her handshake. Honest. She appreciated knowing where she stood with a person straight off, made it much easier when she struggled to catch their words. A few seconds ago, she might have been wrong. Hasty judging was a bad habit.

CHAPTER
SIX

ZIP SPATIAL AWARENESS, but in Winter's boots, Maggie's light stomp on his foot didn't rate more than a tickle. He hadn't been prepared for her to jettison in front of him at that moment. Worried he was standing too close, he stepped back, in case he breathed too hard, and she floated away.

She was small, but that didn't mean much. Most people were. Other than his teammates, who were all similar in height. Thin but gentle curves flattered her delicate body. No make-up. She hadn't worn any yesterday, either. The top of her head barely reached his sternum. Her perfume drifted under his nose. Lemon, lime? Who cared? She smelled great.

But something about the slim interpreter alerted his spidey sense. He hadn't missed her glancing left and right every time they exited an office. She turned and her light blue eyes fixated on his mouth. Sexy as hell unless he had bagel crumbs from breakfast stuck to his chin. As they approached the comms area, he reached across her to punch in the security code. "'Scuse me."

Her eyes sparkled. They did that a lot, and under different circumstances, he'd swear she might be flirting with him. If he wasn't still trying to figure out how to handle Linda without it becoming a major issue he'd have no complaints. Except she had stolen his fucking jacket.

"Where are we?" she asked.

"The comms room. Sentinel's brain." Winter swept his arm across the bank of monitors and equipment covering the entire back wall of the large open space. "Our ears and eyes on the world. It used to be Snake's domain when he worked in the UK. Since he took the lead here in New York, Storm takes care of that aspect of our operation. You'll meet him later."

A row of working desks ran along the left-hand side. "Quiet here now, but there are days when it's busier than Grand Central during rush hour. In here…" He opened a door at the back and led her though into a smaller room. No windows. "The gun safe." No reason to spend time there, so he kept moving.

Maggie didn't ask questions, either. Instead, eyes the color of the sky at that beach in the Bahamas collided with his. Fucking heaven. His lips quirked. "So, you're good with languages?" he asked as they walked along the corridor towards the front door. She had to be way past good for Snake to be impressed.

"Oh, yes. I'm a bit of a nerd. I have a Ph.D. from Columbia. I was lecturing and studying politics at Harvard last year until…"

Winter leaned closer. Almost put his arm around her shoulders. Something had taken the light out of her face, and he didn't like it. Not one bit.

"Until I decided I needed a break. I'm fluent in a bunch of languages and an equal number of dialects. Lip read and can sign in IPSL, Indo-Pakistani Sign Language, which is why Snake reached out to my department head when Sentinel required an interpreter for your next mission. That's what you call it, not a job, right?"

Winter held up his hand. Impressive, but enough with the personal resume. Given the hours she must have spent studying, she didn't have to prove herself to anyone. Brains and beauty. A combo he always admired.

Maggie licked her lips and her focus returned to his mouth. Determined to find that damn crumb, he swiped the corner with the side of his thumb. Her sky-blue eyes widened, sparking his cock's attention.

"I'm sorry. I've forgotten your name. What was it again?" she asked, her cute button nose aimed at the ceiling.

It stung that she didn't remember. "Winter." He scowled. "Yours?" Name swaps at ten paces. Ridiculous, if it wasn't fucking hilarious.

"Do you examine every new employee with microscopic precision, or just the women?" she asked. Her head cocked to the side.

Her question threw him briefly before he laughed. Silent or speaking, Ms. King had a way of catching him off guard. "You're one to talk, lady. You have been staring at my mouth ever since we left the boss' office. *Bit harsh, buddy, but that'll teach her to pick a fight.* Something was up with him. A man who prided himself in his control, staying professional. First Linda, now Ms. King

"I'm sorry."

The sunshine quit her voice. And wasn't he the biggest

schmuck? He went to say forget it and changed tack half-way. "I'll give you a ride home and I can pick up my jacket." Winter held open the comms room door and Maggie ducked under his arm.

He could rescue her, tell her not to worry about the damn coat, but he'd never been Mr. Nice Guy, and he was curious about where she had gone after she ran out on him. Back to Kenny, the dickhead boyfriend?

"Look, I am sorry about yesterday, taking off with your jacket. I…"

"No sweat, but out of interest. Why did you run?"

"I didn't. I got a message from a friend. She had an accident, fell down the stairs, and needed my help."

"Uh-huh. You should have told me. I would have given you a ride. If it was that bad, why did she call you and not 911?"

"Right? I asked her the same thing, and she begged me to come. I would never let a friend down. You were very helpful with Kenny, but I didn't like to impose. Luckily, when I got to her place, the emergency had passed, and she was fine. At that point, calling the paramedics would have been overkill."

What a crock. But why bother questioning it? She should suggest he mind his own business. "Okay. Spare me the details. Let's get moving." The sooner he grabbed his jacket and left her to it, the quicker he could drink the beer sitting in his fridge.

Better still, he could join Trig and Storm downtown, and work off nervous energy. He hadn't gotten laid in months. Perhaps he was getting old because, over the past six months, the whole one-night-stand routine had lost its shine.

"Where do you need to go?" Winter asked, opening the door and signalling for her walk ahead out onto the street.

"Straight across town. The F train gets me there. I'll bring your jacket tomorrow."

"I'm in no hurry." Maggie's gorgeous eyes widened to the size of dinner plates. Eyes incapable of keeping secrets. He did his best not to smirk.

"Er. Did I say across town?"

Wait for it. "You did."

"I meant, way across town, a bridge. In Brooklyn."

Fuck me dead.

"Last night I stayed at a motel, but now that I have a job, I plan on moving to Manhattan, so it's easier to get to work."

"Which motel?"

"Sorry?"

"In Brooklyn. Which motel?"

"The Motor Inn in Red Hook, a short walk from the Smith and Ninth subway. Easy. Look, I don't go around stealing jackets. Kenny freaked me out, I guess, and when I got my friend's call…"

"Shh." Winter shook his head and raised his finger to his mouth. He didn't like liars. Or that Kenny had scared her. But after his experience with Linda, he should do himself a favor and let someone else at Sentinel play Mr Nice Guy. Stay professional. Keep his distance. Except he knew the motel, and there were pockets of the neighborhood he wouldn't let any woman roam alone at night.

Besides, Maggie wasn't to blame for his bad mood. Still being pissed at Snake played a huge part. They didn't have the time or manpower to keep Maggie out of harm's way.

Winter nodded up ahead. "Take the next left. Sentinel parks its vehicles in the alley around back."

Maggie froze. He quickly sidestepped so he didn't send her flying. "Why have you stopped moving?"

"I just remembered. My bag's upstairs. Go ahead, I'll only be a minute."

As she turned, Winter grabbed her elbow. "Wait up. We'll go together."

"What? Why? It's not far."

Took real willpower not to remind her she had a track record when it came to leaving him hanging. "Move."

"Moving," she replied.

Winter laughed.

"Much better," she said.

Her playful smile went a long way to defusing his frustration. "Come on. It's getting late and you must be hungry. My bad, we didn't get to have lunch."

"No. Not hungry. I…"

She looked so damn lost he wanted to tousle her hair. "I insist. There's an okay burger joint close to your motel. We can dump your bag and grab a bite. After all—boss' orders."

Upstairs, George sprawled next to the front desk. Must be waiting for Snake. Anticipating a slobbery welcome, Winter lifted his boot and scraped the toe across the back of his jeans. "Hey, fella. Your buddy Bounce is looking for you."

Ahead, Maggie bent over her bag, her very round, perfectly shaped ass facing him. He strode over, grabbed the handles of her canvas bag, and hauled it over his shoulder. "Hell, what have you got in here?"

She didn't answer, which ticked him off. More fucking secrets. He tapped her wrist. "I said, what's in here?"

"Sorry. I was miles away," she apologized. George closed his eyes, appreciating her scrub under his chin.

"Never mind. Let's go. Otherwise, it will be midnight before we eat. And I'm starving. You must be, too." He'd heard her when she said she wasn't hungry but ignored her. If she had to come on this mission, he didn't want her passing out on him. She needed to keep her body fueled.

By the time they set off again, the rain had stepped up, falling in icy slants across the street. Winter shrugged off his jacket. Déjà vu as he draped it over Maggie's shoulders. But no way would she walk off with a second coat. Before that happened, they'd stop off at Macy's and buy her one.

They turned into the alley. Triple story red brick buildings rose on both sides of the narrow street big enough for a parked car but not two lanes of traffic. Torrents cascaded off the fire escapes and rusted metal shutters covered in graffiti rattled in the wind. The dumpsters overflowing with black garbage bags blocked a few unused loading bays, casting shadows long enough to hide the boogie man. But it was a pretty safe place since only Sentinel and the odd delivery guy needed to access it. Almost at his truck, Maggie tugged on his arm.

"Look. Poor thing."

She trotted after a mongrel cat, scooping the flea-bitten animal into her arms, as the warehouse shutter behind her rolled open and the forklift backed out of it.

"Maggie. Watch out."

No response. Not so much as a fucking blink. This daydreaming sure as shit had to stop. Yelling and waving,

Winter tried to attract her attention above the pounding of the rain. He sprinted after her. "Hey, Maggie. Behind you."

Spinning around, her eyes locked on the forklift. *Damn.* A split second before it hit her, Winter swung his forearm around her waist and lifted her clear of the machine. The cat squawked, leapt from her grasp, and flew off down the alley. The forklift not far behind it.

"What the hell, Maggie? You wanna spend the night in hospital?"

"I didn't hear it. Please. Put me down."

He lowered her to her feet but didn't let go of her, scared shitless she'd end up splattered over the sidewalk. This close, he heard her breathing, could smell the combo of rain and citrus. Understandable, seeing as how she was drenched. Good enough to eat. Until he came to his senses, he had considered nibbling the spot on her neck below her ear. *For fuck's sake.* Hands off. First rule of professional, work colleague, behavior.

Running a hand through his soaked hair, he stated the obvious. "Tomorrow, I'll speak with Snake again, insist you need more time, training, before you're ready to join the team in the field. No way can I have you drifting off in Pakistan. I won't take the risk. With you or my men."

Maggie wrenched out of his hold. Winter didn't need to see the tears glistening in her eyes to know that wasn't what she wanted to hear.

"Please don't. I promise not to be a problem. Let me help you, I can do this. Really, I'm not a ditz. I lost my hearing aid," she blurted.

"'Scuse me?" *Give me a break, sweetheart.*

CHAPTER
SEVEN

MAGGIE ROLLED HER EYES. "Now who's hard of hearing? I lost the damn thing somewhere between Kenny's and the motel. They're very comfortable, but tiny. I didn't notice it had gone until I was at the pier. " Her hands were shaking. She looked around for the forklift. Manhattan wasn't much different from a lot of city downtowns where machinery moved stuff in an out of warehouses. Usually, in the daylight, not the dark.

"Maggie. Stop. Over there. Please, get in the truck." He nodded at the Chevrolet Silverado parked in the alley. Her dad used to drive one. He swore by the vehicle because it could pull his horse trailer. But here in the city, she couldn't help thinking it was overkill. How much did fishing gear weigh?

"Ask Snake if you don't believe me. Why do you think I learned so many types of sign-language?" Did the world need to fall on Winter's head for him to get it? "After I accepted the job, he kindly gave me an advance so I could pick up the new one I've ordered. Which I will, tomorrow.

First thing. Honestly, I swear I'm not an airhead and I can take care of myself. My father taught me to shoot, and I've taken defence classes." Obviously, not convinced. Winter's huff annoyed her.

The night Steve and Josie died, their murderer had punched her hard on the right side of her head, causing permanent damage to her ear. As the prosecution's chief witness her dad had been paranoid Lazenby would come after her. He had insisted she learn how to protect herself. Plus, she'd completed her firearms safety course and had a Massachusetts' License to Carry Permit to prove it.

Many people backed off when they knew she needed a hearing aid. She hated the thing, even though she was used to it. Winter stared at her as if she had two heads, and suddenly it became important the growly bear didn't treat her like she was special, that he believed she could do her job.

In fact, although she had mentioned nothing to him about Lazenby, Snake suggested she apply for her New York Pistol License. Nobody needed to know the detail of her past since—for now—it was still her past.

Looking as though he would insist, Winter ran his hand through his hair, and rolled his shoulders back so she spread her feet wider, determined to fight for her spot on the Sentinel team.

"Why didn't you say anything? No, I blame myself," he grumbled. "I knew something wasn't right."

Maggie sighed and considered grabbing his hand. How whacked was that? Touching a bad-tempered bear wouldn't help prove her capabilities, so she dropped her arm to her side.

"Okay, Let's start again, Winter. You give me that ride. I apologize as many times as you want for taking your coat and return it. Over that burger you suggested, we agree that tomorrow, when we see each other, we start fresh. What do you say? Deal?" One hand behind her back, fingers crossed, she offered her other to shake on it.

Damn. When he hesitated a beat too long, her heart leapt to her throat, afraid he'd decided not to give her that chance. If it took begging, she might be willing for this job and salary. Maggie raised her chin.

"Deal." Winter's ginormous hand swamped hers. Sparks of electricity zapped the hairs on her arm, making her flinch. "Er, did you notice where the kitty went?" She gulped. The skinny alley cat must have gotten the shock of its life. All skin and bone, it looked as though it hadn't eaten in days.

"Don't worry about the damned animal. More to the point, I'd like to know what near-sighted ass drove that forklift."

If the way Winter glared at her meant he expected an answer, he was out of luck. She shivered. The forklift was long gone and she refused to consider trouble may have followed her from Boston.

"You're soaked. Come on, get in the truck." Winter opened the door.

One foot on the step, she was half in when two hands firmly clasped her hips and plopped her into her seat. Dumbstruck, she watched him stride around to the driver's side, climb in, start the engine, and immediately switch on the heat. A bonus because her toes were icicles. If she wiggled them, they'd snap.

She turned to get a better look at the man who, one

50

minute, had to be the scariest person on the planet, a grizzly bear, and the next, made sure she didn't freeze.

"You like what you see?" he asked, raising an eyebrow.

"Very much." Taking a breath for courage, she kept right on staring.

"Oh yeah, and why's that?"

"Well. You are my hero. Yesterday, you rescued me from Kenny and today here you are saving me from being run over by a forklift and washed away by the rain." Maggie ran her hand over the steamed up windshield. "Looks like it's set in for the evening." She forced a smile. Rain or snow didn't bother her most of the time, but another night sleeping in the park would be more than uncomfortable. Keeping her clothes dry, impossible. Turning up at the airport tomorrow looking like a drowned rat would crucify her credibility.

One good thing. Last night, between seeing Lazenby in every flickering shadow and the noise from the expressway, a few blocks over, she hadn't slept. No reason it would be different tonight. That meant in the morning, catching the early subway wouldn't be a problem. And she didn't need to swing by Penn Station either. Sentinel's locker room had a shower. Releasing her grip from the edge of her seat, she leaned her head back and tried to relax.

"Thoughts?" Winter beeped his horn and swerved to avoid a drunk stumbling across the road.

"I was wondering what happens before we leave for Pakistan." The truck's tires swished through a puddle, splashing water up over the sidewalk.

"I'll pick you up at seven tomorrow. Snake will hold a final briefing at Sentinel before we head to the plane. Fill everyone in on the latest intel and make any last-minute changes to the current game plan. You will meet the Trigger and Storm, plus the rest of the team."

"Sounds good."

Winter frowned but couldn't stop his lips twitching. Maggie swore he was trying not to laugh. Guess it had been a dumb choice of words. At least he hadn't mentioned her staying behind again.

Things had to get better. Living in Boston, working at the university, had been her happy place, always thought she'd stay there forever, marry an academic who wore glasses and never ironed his shirts. Her apartment had been a short walk from where she lectured and studied and every day she commuted in daylight.

Nothing like her upside down existence now. Knowing Lazenby had escaped, was out there somewhere on the streets, had rattled her. The job with Sentinel meant she could save some money and decide what to do next. Pakistan might not be her top choice for a hiding place, but the chances of Lazenby looking for her there had to be zero. Best scenario the police would capture him while she was gone. In the meantime, she could use her skills to help bring those kidnapped women home.

"Don't worry, Maggie. I won't leave your side. Tomorrow, can I send Linda to pick up the…" He tugged on his earlobe.

"The hearing aid. Go ahead, say it. I'm not offended." She tried not to giggle and ended up snorting.

"Sorry. I deserved that." He reached over and opened the glove compartment. "There should be some gloves in there.

Put them on. They'll stop you from getting frostbite until the truck warms up."

"Thanks, and I shouldn't have been snarky. It's a kind offer, picking up the aid, but I need to make sure it fits properly."

"Okay. But if you need anything else, sing out, and Linda will be all over it."

Linda? She had to think for a minute. Lack of sleep had made her brain foggy. "Ah yes, your new receptionist. I bet she's super together. Her and Sam." Unlike her. Not now. Once upon a time, before Steve's murder.

Leaving Boston had been a real drag, but waking every morning and not knowing whether her cell had another ten missed calls with no message, or if she'd find more plants knocked off the window ledge had put her nerves on edge. First the fire, then the break-in had been the final straw. At work, she hardly ever made a mistake, but she'd started messing up big time.

"You're right about Sam, for sure," Winter agreed, his voice pulling her away from the depressing memory. "The boss' wife is ex-military and an ace K9 trainer."

Maggie rubbed the back of her teeth with the tip of her tongue and thought how great it must feel to be admired like that, especially by Winter.

"When you work for Sentinel, you join a large family. We all are here for each other. Anything you need. Ask and me, any of us, will be glad to help."

She didn't expect him to grasp her forearm. His reassuring squeeze completely threw her. After feeling alone for a long time, his words brought tears to the corner of her eyes. "Thanks. So, Winter, when you're not saving the world, what do you like to do besides fishing?" she said, trying to lighten the conversation.

"Fishing's enough for me." He let go of her arm, taking a small part of his comfort with him. "You? What floats your boat?" he asked with a chuckle. Low and soft, the tone encouraging.

"Dancing. I love to dance. Boot scoot, or tango, around my living room. When I lived in Boston, I belonged to a group. We met three times a week in a hall a few blocks from the university. I miss it," she confessed.

There were plenty of nightclubs in Manhattan. Kenny had tried to have her to go with him. He didn't get that was the place she couldn't dance. Being Steve's best friend, knowing her brother had been killed outside a club, he should have understood. Another gush of water hit the window. Bigger, louder, it made her jump and crash against Winter's side. "Sorry, I wasn't expecting it."

She folded her arms. Exhausted, she gave up and stopped babbling. Vaguely, she was aware they'd entered the downtown tunnel, and as the inside of the truck got darker, so did her world.

"Hey, wake up. We're here." Winter spun the wheel and parked in front of the motel.

Maggie shook her head. She couldn't have been asleep long, but there was a thickness behind her eyeballs, like someone had stuffed a thousand pillows inside her skull. "Wait here. Let me grab your jacket."

"I'll come with you. I need to stretch my legs." Winter offered.

Before she could stop him, Winter had strode to her side of the vehicle and opened her door. Same as before, he lifted her out of her seat and onto the sidewalk. "You can wait in the lobby. I won't be long."

Inside, Winter wandered over and sat in one of the red chairs shaped like a giant peanut. "Now that's surreal." Maggie giggled.

"Hey, don't mock. Go. Hurry. I'm starving."

Maggie took a second longer, watching him before she stepped out of sight into the public restroom. Finding an empty stall, she put her bag on the floor, pulled out Winter's jacket, and returned to where she'd left him. "Here you are. First thing I'll do when I'm paid is have it dry cleaned. Don't let me forget."

"No need. Come on. Let's go get food."

"Sorry, it's been a long day. Can I take a rain check? I want to be fully awake and fresh tomorrow." Like that was possible, but if he found out where she intended to spend the night, all bets would be off, and she'd be jobless.

"Sure. No problem. Rain check it is. Goodnight, Maggie. See you in the morning."

Far out. Maggie sighed. Relieved that Winter hadn't forced her to eat, she rushed back to the restroom and collected her bag.

To be certain he'd left, she waited five minutes before leaving the motel. Drawing in a breath, she braced against the rain ricocheting off the buildings. Her feet squelched in her shoes as she failed to avoid the large puddles. Walking fast up Hamilton Avenue, she kept looking over her shoulder, sure someone was following her.

Paranoid much? But after Detective Esposito's call, her stomach hadn't quit rolling with the same unease she'd experienced in Boston when stuff got scary. The bone-chilling cold deep under her skin had nothing to do with the weather.

CHAPTER
EIGHT

WINTER THUMPED the truck's steering wheel with the heel of his hand. He must be getting soft in his old age. Fresh start. For fuck's sake. Tinkerbelle. Could he object? No. He'd traveled to hell and back more than once in his career, but the optimism in Maggie's Bahama blue eyes stripped him of his courage.

She made it plain—no special treatment. Except no one with a hearing issue belonged where they were going. She claimed she could handle a weapon. He'd check with the boss, but most likely, another fairy tale.

Bottom line, Maggie was a civilian who had no business being in the middle of what might be open combat. He had a duty to make sure she stayed out of harm's way. Winter pulled his cell out of his pocket and called the boss. *Come on, Snake, answer your damn phone.* He drummed his fingers on his knee and rehearsed his case until the ringtone flipped to voice mail.

Sam wouldn't be happy when he showed up on their doorstep, but there wasn't a lot he could do about that.

Winter turned the key in the ignition. The engine purred to life as a familiar emerald-green beanie on a particular pretty head exited the motel. If she'd changed her mind and wanted a burger, great. Except why the hell was she hauling her entire suitcase behind her?

A heavy curtain of rain hung over the street. Visibility almost zero except for the one bare bulb above the doorway. Not that it would have made any difference if it was broad daylight. With zip situational awareness, not bothering to look around her, Maggie hurried along the sidewalk. Watching from behind, he had the advantage, but she had no idea a dark blue Buick coasted a couple of hundred yards behind her.

Could be nothing. A lost driver, slowing to check Google maps, but in his world, shit was rarely that simple. Winter jumped from his truck; eyes glued to her as she turned the corner. Passing headlights picked up the blond braid swinging in the wind, making her easier to see as she headed off along Hamilton Avenue. He followed at a discreet distance. Five minutes later, Maggie hopped the fence of a small park.

Staying close enough not to lose sight of her wasn't easy. Difficult to see much beyond the end of his nose through the deluge pounding the open space. If not for the lights from a passing car, he might have lost her. Visible in the corner, under a clump of trees, her slight frame crouched over her bag and pulled out a goddam hoodie, rolled it into a ball and hugged it against her chest.

Rain cascaded off a hanging branch above her head. Winter shivered in sympathy. With a yelp, Maggie's head spun in his direction. *Damn.* Sure, she'd made him, he ducked behind a hedge and watched the shadows jumping at odd angles in the space between them. In case any unwanted company had joined them, Winter checked the gun in his hip holster.

"Who's there?"

Surprisingly, her voice didn't waver. He stayed quiet. Didn't feel great not answering her, but if his instincts were correct, and they were seldom wrong, he wasn't about to alert whoever else might be lurking in the dark that he was there.

"Please? I know you're there. Come out where I can see you."

Maggie stared directly at him. *Aw shit.* Bad guys, go fuck yourself, because he couldn't handle the shake in her voice, the fear vibrating off her. "It's me. Winter." He stepped out and widened his stance, ready to hop which-ever way she dodged. Shield her with his body, but she swung the hoodie over her shoulders, crossed her ankles and sat on the soaked grass. "What the hell are you doing?"

"Why are you following me? You scared me."

"Yeah. Apologies. I saw you leave the motel and…"

"And what? You have your coat. We agreed. Fresh start. Tomorrow.

She sniffed. Water ran down the front of her neck and disappeared under her top. Winter exhaled. Impossible to be sure, could be another vagrant trying to find a bed for the night, but as far as he could tell, whoever had intended to keep Maggie company tonight had changed their mind.

"Go home, back to Manhattan, or wherever, and leave me alone," she said.

Bossy, determined. He liked this side of her, but… "I can't do that, Maggie. Why are you here?"

"I live here."

"No way." His jaw dropped to his boots as his blood pressure climbed.

"Yes, way. Oh, this is ridiculous. Following people around. Don't you ever leave work? Go fishing somewhere else. The slimy, scaly kind. Duh, hero. Work-life balance. Take a break from the day job occasionally. Otherwise, you are heading for an early grave, mister." Maggie's arms flew out wide and the hoodie landed in a puddle. "Damn. Now look what you made me do."

Winter dropped to his knee and scooped the thin hoodie out of the rain. "Hell, lady, tell me you are not planning on spending the night here. You will catch your death if someone doesn't cut your throat first."

"Jeez. I didn't figure you for a drama queen. I slept here yesterday. Alone. Saw no one." She snapped her fingers.

"Put that down to luck more than good sense, sweetheart. Here, you're soaked. Take my jacket."

"Not this again. I don't want your coat. Mine will do fine." Maggie snatched her hoodie from his hand.

"Okay. Easy. No coat. I get it. What else can I do to help?"

"Simple! Go away."

"No can do, sweetheart. It would be downright irresponsible leaving you here. I live close by. How about we go back to the motel, grab my truck, and I'll take you to my place? Stay in my spare room tonight. It has its own bathroom. Grab a hot shower and something to eat. You can leave your bag there. Safe, while we're in Pakistan."

Maggie eased her grip on the hoodie, and he hoped he

was getting through to her. "When we get back, I'll help you find a decent place to live. In the meantime, how about you tell me what the hell is going on? Did you even notice the Buick following you?" Squinting through the rain, she scanned the park. "Didn't think so." Exasperated, he slapped his hand on his thigh.

"Okay. No need to shout."

Hair plastered to her head, water dripping off her nose, she managed a half-smile and he'd never wanted to kiss anyone more his entire life. Seeing Maggie determined not to fall apart, giving him hell for interfering while she did her best not to shiver, aroused every one of his protector instincts. And he didn't need help from his cock, nudging his zipper to tell him how much he would like to get to know her a whole lot better. The woman was too young. At a wild guess, also too inexperienced, to handle his idea of bedroom play.

He straightened his knee, rose to his full height, and picked up her sodden canvas bag. Unsure about following him, but she did, mainly because she didn't want to lose her stuff? He'd carried the thing more in the last forty-eight hours than his own damn pack. Winter reached for her hand, praying she'd take it. Attached to him, she was safe. Plus, she might think twice before running away. He was more than over that bull crap. But the woman had other ideas, shrugging out of his grip and taking a step away from him.

As they left the park, he eyeballed the street. *There you are, fucker.* Difficult in the dark, but he took a mental picture for Storm. If he ran the scan and confirmed it was Kenny, he might have to pay shit for brains a visit. And he would be lying if he said breaking Kenny's nose didn't appeal. "You expecting anyone to meet you?" he asked, trying to keep his voice steady.

"No." The casual, high-pitched ring in her tone bordered on comedic.

"Oh, I don't know. The furtive glances you're tossing over your shoulder every three seconds. Who is it?"

"Furtive? Jeez, Winter. Where did you pick up such a broad vocabulary?"

"Claws in, sweetheart. I went to college."

"Really?" That hurt. Maggie sounded genuinely surprised. "What was your major?"

"Nursing." His answer stopped her dead in her tracks, and she burst out laughing. The sound tickled him in all the right places, but as much as he wanted to play, make her laugh some more, he took hold of her elbow and kept them moving.

"Nursing. Are you joking?" She wiggled from his grip and almost fell.

Seeing as she had refused to take his hand, he offered his arm, like his mother had taught him, and hell if his heartbeat didn't steady when she wrapped her thin arm around his massive biceps. Hours in the gym paid off.

Latched onto him, there was no danger of her falling. "No. Topped my class. You saying you don't believe me?" He winked, glad when her face softened. He raised his hand and gently swiped the rain from her forehead and cheek. "You skin is beautif…" *Fuck me.* Winter cleared his throat.

Head cocked to one side, lines creasing her smooth forehead, Maggie finished the job and brushed her hair behind her ear. "That's fantastic, Winter. Nursing, I'd never have guessed. More men should go into the profession. I was, er, in an accident when I was a kid, and I spent a month in the hospital."

She squeezed her eyes shut for a second against the wind. He pulled her closer, loving the way her body fit against his hip. *Don't want her to trip.* His brain rushed in, trying to prevent him from getting any closer to the gigantic mistake of kissing her.

"After it happened, an awesome male nurse sat with me when I had nightmares, didn't leave until I fell asleep. Why did you quit?" Maggie swung sideways to avoid the puddle.

For a second, the light that constantly poured out of her dimmed, trickled with the rain from her face, dragging his heart along with it. *What had happened?* Clearly, she wasn't about to spill right now, with the wind howling under the expressway.

"I said, why did you stop nursing?" Maggie tugged on his sleeve.

"I didn't." Winter said, his eyes fixed across the street on another shift in the shadows. Whoever was following them had stepped out of their vehicle. The person was medium build, but a distinctly male silhouette. Hands in his pocket, collar close to his ears, he stood across the street, watching.

CHAPTER
NINE

MAGGIE HURRIED to keep up with Winter. "Didn't what?" She circled her hand, encouraging him to keep talking. The rain and the wind worked overtime, drowning out most sound. If she had any hope of hearing him, she couldn't risk losing sight of his lips.

"Didn't stop nursing," Winter answered. His head angled towards her, but his gaze landed across the street. "Never started. I studied civil engineering at West Point. Strictly steel and bricks. There isn't an empathetic bone in my body." His lips quirked.

The promise of a dimple made him more handsome. If that was possible. "Oh." Maggie shook her head. Disappointed, but not surprised.

Winter looked nothing like the nurse who had helped her in the hospital after Steve's murder. His massive chest owned every crease of his leather jacket, and his long legs stretched the seams of his denim jeans to prowling perfection.

Every powerful inch of him hollered warrior. A good

thing, because she was ninety percent certain the car Winter mentioned was the same one she had seen last night outside the park. She hadn't mentioned it before in case he twisted it around to support his argument for not letting her come to Pakistan.

As they approached his truck, Winter guided her to the passenger side. The wind fought back as she tried to open the door.

"Here, allow me." Winter reached around her and opened it.

After helping her climb in, he jogged to the driver's side, turned the key in the ignition, and they were on their way. As it was crazy speaking over the deluge pounding the hood, she didn't bother.

Winter kept glancing in his rear-view mirror, which made her nervous. Refusing to believe Lazenby had found her, Maggie pinched the bridge of her nose and told herself it was the lousy weather playing tricks on her, encouraging her imagination to work overtime, making her see stuff in the shadows. There were no zombies, waving axes, lurching across the street.

She took a deep breath and focussed on her hands. Keeping them low, she started signing, practicing key sentences and phrases that might be useful when she questioned Adnan. A how-to-interrogate-a-kidnapper phrase book would be useful right now.

They had been driving for a while when Winter turned to her and asked, "What was that?" He nodded at her hands and adjusted his mirror.

It helped to speak as well as sign. "Sorry, I'm brushing up on my Farsi."

"How do you do it?" he said, pointing at her hands.

"Do what?"

"Remember," he continued, as they sped up around a corner.

Maggie watched the window wipers beat faster and shrugged. "Lucky, I guess. Words are musical, so every language had its own set of friendly ear worms."

"Hang on." His arm swung in front of her, pinning her to her seat as he swerved and headed down a side street.

Already on edge, her nerves ratcheted up a notch. She gripped the edge of her seat. "Umm. If I have a problem, I recite poetry, try to find a rhythm. Make sense?"

"Sounds complicated."

Talk about made of iron. Even though they were driving way too fast, Winter's face showed no sign of concern. Except for the twitch in the corner of his eye. But if he could handle it, so could she. *Ha!* "I love poetry. My brother and I used to make up nonsense all the time, but his stuff was the best." Her voice hitched.

"Was?"

Winter raised an eyebrow, and for the first time since they left the park, his face didn't look as though it had lost its battery. "Yes. He died."

"I'm sorry for your loss."

Silently thanking the stars that he wasn't pushing for more, Maggie let out the breath she'd been holding. Not wanting Winter to see her cry, she turned to look out the window. "What do you like to read?" she asked, trying not to sniff.

"I don't. Prefer to watch the movie version. You okay?"

"Fine thanks. And you're wrong."

"What? You think the book is always better?" He spun the wheel, and the truck screeched to a halt alongside the curb.

Surprised by the unexpected water hitting her window, Maggie lurched sideways and instinctively reached for Winter's solid thigh. "Er, sorry," she mumbled and slid her palm from his lap. "Of course, books are better, but I meant the bit about you not being empathetic. You are a very caring person."

Immediately feeling like an idiot for letting her mouth run ahead of her brain, she waited for a smart remark, but Winter didn't say a word until he'd made it around to her side, opened her door, and ducked his head inside.

"There you go again with the bull crap, Maggie King. Talk to me after we return from Pakistan. I'll expect a revised sitrep."

She glanced over Winter's shoulder as he helped her out of the truck and was relieved when she saw no sign of the Buick. Kenny didn't own a car. Jeez, Detective Esposito had spooked her. Before she showered, she'd call him and get an update on Lazenby.

Winter frowned. "What is it?"

"Nothing. Is this your place?" She nodded at the impressive brownstone.

"It is." His frown deepened.

Maggie suspected he wouldn't stop digging until she gave in and told him everything, including her brother's murder. It wasn't a secret. Mr. Google could supply every detail. But whenever she spoke about Steve and Josie, she got depressed for days. Falling into a funk before they left for Pakistan was a risk she couldn't take.

"Watch your step." Winter tilted his chin at the uneven sidewalk.

Maggie chuckled, disappointed he didn't offer his arm this time. "It's okay, Winter. It's my ear that's stuffed, not my feet."

He grinned.

"A smile. Wow!" She pressed the side of her hand against her forehead, shielded her face from the rain to get a better look, loving the way his eyes crinkled.

"Come on. It's too cold to hang around out here. We both could use a shower and food." He placed the palm of his hand against her back and nudged her up the stone stairs.

How water sounded like heaven, but the warmth of Winter's touch radiating along her spine rated a great second. At the top, their bodies swayed into each other, and his black eyes flared. So, what? That couldn't mean a damn thing except shock horror at the hair plastered to her head. The smudged mascara running down her cheek. She must look a complete disaster. Heck, her nose dripped like a faucet.

Winter lifted her chin. The heat of his gaze blazed through her and snatched her breath. *Kiss me.*

CHAPTER
TEN

"MAGGIE, I..." Winter cleared his throat and told himself that he was more than his dick. Kissing the pretty girl in a downpour, while violins played in the background, happened only in the movies, but Maggie stared at his mouth, and he was captivated by the pulse beating at the side of her long neck.

A novice mistake, when he should be keeping his fucking eyes peeled for the guy in the Buick. On cue, the fucker charged out of the dark and opened fire.

Winter threw his body against Maggie's, pinning her to the door of the brownstone. Too exposed at the top of the stairs, he grabbed her arms, made sure he covered her completely, and braced for the second shot. But their attacker wasn't hanging around. He took off down the street as though the hounds of hell were chasing him.

"Winter," Maggie gasped.

Like him, she wanted answers he didn't have. Not yet. Her hands dragged across the red streaks slashed across her ghost white face. Christ! Terrified she was hit, he punched in the code. His palm on top of her head, his front glued to her back, he nudged her into the house and kicked the door shut.

He cursed when she stumbled, fearing she'd taken a bullet meant for him, which, given his line of work, was more than likely. There wasn't much chance of a breach into his home, but what had happened with Smiley had taught him to never say never.

He bundled her upstairs to his office, safest place in the house, and because he needed to feel her close, he hooked one arm around her waist, swung the other under her knees and scooped her into his arms.

Immediately, she buried her head into his chest and clung to him. Taking the stairs two at a time, he made it to his office and laid her on the couch next to the wall-to-ceiling bookcase. He'd lied when he said he preferred movies to books. Three-D, hold in your hand stories crammed the shelves.

"Talk to me. Where are you hit?" Heart pounding, he carefully patted the front of her shirt.

"I'm not sure," she gasped. "Nothing hurts."

Not always a good sign. She could be in shock. The red patches under his fingers weren't sticky, didn't have the tell-tale metallic smell of blood. Because it wasn't blood. Rage swiftly followed his initial relief. Maggie's eyelids fluttered. "Hey, it's okay. It's paint. Look." He wiggled his hand in front of her. A dumbass idea. Maggie's breath hitched, and her eyes rolled to the ceiling. "No, no, no." He gently tapped the side of her cheeks. "Stay with me, sweetheart."

She pointed at the bookcase. "I thought you said you preferred movies."

The smile usually tucked behind her voice had vanished. "I lied. Rest. I'll get you some water."

"No. Wait. Please." Maggie clawed the sleeve of his jacket.

"Hey, relax. I'll stay." Winter slowly uncurled her fingers. She was safe here. He ought to check outside, make sure the guy had kept on running and not swung back for another go at his target, except a violent attack always left you wondering if you were the only person who'd survived. In his case, it had been true.

No way could he leave her. He'd stay 'til she settled. Checking her pulse, Winter rubbed the pad of his thumb along the inside of her wrist. A little on the speedy side, but that was to be expected. Inside, he shook like Jello on a plate.

"What happened?" She closed her eyes and swallowed hard.

"You took the words out of my mouth, sweetheart." Whoever paint balled them hadn't planned on killing anyone. Getting shot at was a routine part of his day job, but the seconds until he'd confirmed Maggie wasn't wounded had scared the bejesus out of him. "Could be some local punk kids, unless you have any idea who it was?" Worth a shot. If she did, it would make it a lot easier finding the creep.

"Why are you asking me? I don't know."

Odd, the hitch in her voice, so he pushed. "Could it be your ex? Kenny? Don't worry, I'll make sure he doesn't get within three feet of you ever again."

"No. He's creepy, weird, but not violent. And he's never been my boyfriend." Tears streamed down her face, and he didn't have the heart to argue.

"Okay." He'd check the footage from the security camera above the door. Later they'd talk more. After he got some food into her, and she'd slept. "Still nauseous?"

"No. Not so much. Do you live here alone?" she asked, climbing off the sofa and wobbling over to the bookshelves.

"Yep." Alone with his demons, his privacy meant a lot to him. Sharing his home had never appealed. But now he'd met Maggie, a small piece of him, buried way down deep in his gut, poked its head over Smiley's shadow.

Maggie explored the shelf, picking up his grandfather's old travel clock before he could ask her not to touch it. She wouldn't drop it. Until she did.

"Yikes. I'm sorry, Winter. Say it isn't broken."

She crouched and gathered it from the bare wooden floor. Her fingers trembled under his as he helped her stand and slipped the clock from her shaky grip. "No harm done." Maggie's forehead fell against his chest, her nose buried deep against his pec.

"I really am sorry," she whispered.

He tucked an arm around her shoulder and gave her a hug. Her sniffles threatened to open parts of him he'd kept rigid and closed for the best part of a decade.

Aroused by their closeness, he took hold of the tops of her arms and eased her away. Still pale, but there was more color in her cheeks. "It's only a clock. Come on. I'll show you your room so you can rest." Winter placed the only thing left of his grandfather back on the shelf, promising he'd check for cracks later.

Moving ahead, he was careful not to turn his back on her. She had a much better chance of hearing if she could see his

72

face. His mouth. He got it now. First thing tomorrow, Maggie King would have her damn hearing aid.

Downstairs, Winter stopped outside and to his left. "This is yours. Your bathroom's through there." His arm skimmed her chest as he pointed to the area behind the staircase. "Beyond that is the door to the back yard. Don't worry, it's locked. I'll give you the codes."

"Winter?" Maggie murmured.

He'd rescued enough people from dangerous situations to understand she might be in shock. "Yeah?" Nothing else would happen. He'd make sure of it.

"Where do you sleep?" Her cheeks flushed. Her lips parted.

Right beside you. If you let me. "Across the hall. The kitchen is back upstairs. Go freshen up, and I'll fix us something to eat. If you prefer, I can bring you a tray. Leave you in peace." He forced a smiled.

"Thanks, but I'd rather not be alone. I'll just be a minute and join you. Where's my bag?"

"Wait here. I'll fetch it." Not wanting to leave her standing there looking so damned lost, he hurried to where he'd left it. By the front door, Maggie's earlier screams rang in his ears. Those red streaks on her face and hoodie churned in his gut as he returned to her side. "Here. You sure you're okay?"

"Yes. Better now. Thanks for inviting me to stay tonight."

"It's all good." Maggie had no way of knowing, but he wasn't letting her out of his sight. Maybe, big, fucking maybe, when they found the paintballer, he would stop at breaking his arm.

CHAPTER
ELEVEN

MAGGIE STOOD next to the chest of drawers, still a little shaky, but feeling a lot better than she had fifteen minutes ago. The room was big, but not overwhelming. A cream comforter and two pillows covered the bed and looked a lot more inviting than Kenny's.

After the crass way he'd acted on the pier, it didn't surprise her that Winter thought Kenny might be the jerk who'd sprayed them with paint, but like she'd said, it wasn't the kind of thing Kenny would do. Too much of a coward to get that close.

She wouldn't be here very long, but she pulled her clothes out for tomorrow and hung them up in the small closet, hoping they'd lose some of their creases. Given the weather and the drama of the last hour, she had to reek of b.o. A hot shower would also help her lose the chills, but the bathroom was too scary close to the back door.

An extra squirt of her deodorant, before she changed into some dry clothes, would have to do until she got used to the creaks and groans of the old brownstone and found the courage to take that shower.

Exhausted, it took more effort than it should to place one leg in her jeans before lifting the other. Blue dots swam in front of her. Luckily, her hand found the wall before she sprawled across the floor. Along with her hearing loss came iffy balance. But this was way more. Her breath locked in her chest.

Positive she heard a gun fire, Maggie's hands flew to her head. *"Run!" Steve yelled.* The door was shut. No one was there. She clutched her throat and bit the inside of her cheek. Reality check. *This is not then. This is now. Breathe.* She repeated the words, like the counselor had told her. Gradually, the room stopped spinning and she could suck in a long, deep breath.

Winter was worried about her sleeping in the park and had insisted his place was much safer than Red Hook. Hard to believe when idiots ran round his neighborhood paint-balling random strangers, but it had to be the local crazy or kids. Lazenby preferred the real deal to a pretend gun. Slowly, she finished dressing. Food didn't appeal, but she did not want to be alone.

She couldn't see any radiators, but the house was warm, so she left her soaked shoes next to the bed to dry. Exhausted, feeling more eighty-five, than twenty-five, Maggie clutched the banister and hauled herself up the stairs to Winter's kitchen.

A heavy wooden counter with a marble top stood in the center of the room. The super-tech food processor sitting at one end looked like it could take her to the moon, and the block of sharp knives next to it hollered dangerous.

Judging by the many shiny black cupboards, the multi-burner cooker and double fridge, a serious chef worked here. Could be Winter, but between rescuing the world and fishing, where would he find the time? Most likely, a girl-friend or a wife. Someone who would be home any minute disappointed they had an unexpected guest.

Winter had his back to her, talking on his cell as he pulled eggs and salad stuff out of the fridge. Figuring it must be the police, she wanted to hear what he was saying.

"Okay, boss, but other than Maggie speaks a zillion languages, what else did our routine employee check say?"

Curious why he was checking up on her, Maggie froze inside the doorway.

"Damn right I have a problem. You know I am worried about taking a civilian on this next job. Of course, I trust you, but I'm not so sure we can rely on Ms. King. And if my instincts are correct, some fool just tried to take her out with a paintball gun!"

Son of a... Preparing to show herself and give Winter a piece of her mind, Maggie curled her fingers into fists.

"Now we're on the same page. What the actual fuck is right," Winter continued. "We were outside my place. And before you ask, it's for sure not what you are thinking. I'd like answers. Exactly who is this woman? How about we have Storm do a full security work up? Bottom line, I want to know who Maggie King is, and if she was the target, why?"

Well, that hurt. Maggie swallowed the enormous boulder lodged in her throat and turned to leave as the fridge door closed.

"Shit. I'll call you back, boss. Hey, wait up," Winter yelled after her.

She might be tired, but she sprinted down the stairs and slammed against the front door. *Think, Maggie, think.* If Winter was right and she was the target, one foot outside and she'd step into their hands.

Instead, she cut to the bedroom, flew to the opposite side of the bed, her back to the wall. Hidden in the darkness behind her closed eyes, she willed herself to stay calm and not overreact. "Don't do that, Maggie." She thumped the sides of her head with her fists. Overthinking stuff was a curse. She always ended up too far along a road she should never have taken.

Winter didn't trust her, and damn him, it mattered. At her interview she hadn't lied, hadn't gone into a lot of detail. When he'd found her in the park, she probably should have told him why she left Boston, especially as he'd been kind and offered her a place to stay. But fewer people knowing who she was, meant less chance of Lazenby finding her.

Maybe Kenny? He was mad at her for leaving, mainly because he had to pay the rent. But violent? No. Creepy? Hell, yes. She shivered.

Breathe. The gigantic sigh ought to make her feel better. All the self-help books claimed it would. Until she hyper-ventilated, like the last time, and her head floated off into the ether. Had she felt more in control? A big fat, no.

Trying to figure out what to do next, she forced arms by her side. For sure, she couldn't stay at Winter's. The sharp knock rattled her teeth.

"Maggie."

What did Winter want? Nothing more to say. He'd made

it super clear to Snake that she didn't belong on the job, and why would anything she said change his mind? "Go away." She shifted closer to the wall. Another knock. This one louder, more insistent.

"Can I come in?"

"It's your house." That was petty. She tried again. "Sure."

Winter's enormous frame filled the doorway. She longed to be that big. No one messed with a body that had to angle sideways to make it through the doorway. In the center of his shirt there was a splodge of red, which made him look like an extra from a vampire movie. Even though the day couldn't get any worse, Maggie smiled.

Making no move to come any closer, he scratched the stubble on his chin. It must itch, but she hoped he didn't shave, not yet, because he owned the mountain man thing. Plus, the lips he rolled together. Darn, she may be mad at him, but his sharp intake of breath before he spoke stirred something low in her belly.

"Sorry. I didn't mean for you to hear that."

"S'okay. I get it. The girl who steals coats. I wouldn't trust me either." The fishbone stuck in her throat threatened to crucify any control over her tears. "I'm leaving. Tell Snake, thanks for offering me the job, but I understand that I'm not suited for it." She swiped at her tears, feeling more stupid than sad, but it didn't matter how hard she blinked, she couldn't focus. Her hands fumbled with the zipper on her bag.

"Hold up. Snake hasn't fired you, and you are not walking out of here tonight. A ton of reasons before you ask. Let's settle for it's too damn late, and some crazy fuck is getting his kicks shooting innocent people with paint. All I want is an honest answer to my questions. No crap. You think you can do that?"

Depends. Unlikely, if he expected her to spill her full, sad story. "I'll do my best."

"That's a start. Food is almost ready. Come back upstairs. We'll talk while we eat." The tone in his voice left no room to disagree.

She waited a few minutes, then stepped into the hall and took another look at the front door. Unlike Kenny's place, it didn't have a heavy-duty Fox lock.

"Maggie. You coming?" Winter peered over the rail at the top of the stairs.

Why not? She hadn't eaten a proper meal since the night she left Kenny's, and talking some more with Winter might help her decide what to do. Foot on the bottom stair, she took a last look into her room and out the opposite window. Outside, the warm glow from the bridge lights shone between the houses and glistened on the raindrops.

She hadn't noticed before, but someone had lined the walls of the staircase with old album covers. They were dog-eared and fading. Hanging halfway up, the cover for Coltrane's Blue Train was the only one in a frame. Winter, or was it his wife, liked jazz? Somehow, cowboy boots, fishing, and all, she imagined Winter more of a country music kind of guy.

"Sit." Winter waved a wooden spoon at the gigantic oak dining table in the center of the kitchen and strode over, carrying two white bowls. "Hope you eat pasta?"

"I do. Thanks. Smells delicious." Her stomach growled.

"When did you last eat?" he asked.

"This morning." A pretzel she'd grabbed from the guy outside the subway.

Gorgeous, caring, and the man cooked. What heaven let Winter loose? Without a wife. He rolled his eyes, and she wondered what it would be like if this wasn't pity pasta, more of a dinner date. The exact same time her obsessed brain shouted, ludicrous. A man as sexy and together as Winter could never be interested in a flake who lived on the street and stole coats.

"There's plenty of salad." He shoved a glass bowl brimming with healthy greens towards her.

Maggie waved at the fridge. "Any chance of a drink?"

"Sure. What would you like? Water, wine?" He raised an eyebrow.

"Oh, I see what you're trying to do. You think alcohol will loosen my tongue and I'll spill. Tell you all my secrets. You must be Sentinel's top negotiator."

"No. The sniper."

CHAPTER
TWELVE

WINTER KEPT EATING while Maggie pushed the last of her food around the plate. Each lazy lift of her fork reflected how much the past hour had taken from her. Exhaustion blurred the sparkle in her eyes and her skin was ashen. Before she crashed, she ought to eat three times as much as she had, but he wasn't about to force feed her.

He wanted to apologize, but for what? Taking her to Pakistan was too big a risk, even if their job would be a great deal harder without her skills. For different reasons, they both were tongue-tied. Must need sleep, too, because he considered kissing her. The best way to ease the tightness in her jaw. Would she let him? He'd vote no. She was still mad at him.

Make-up sex could be hot. Alternatively, he could sit by her bed, read her a damn poem, an entire book of them, if it took relaxed her enough to fall asleep. Forgive him?

Winter pushed back his plate and stood. "Follow me," he murmured and reached for her hand. As her eyes were half-closed, he didn't want her falling down the stairs.

"Huh?" Maggie yawned and leaned into the back of her chair.

"Hand. Bed." No sense confusing Sleepy with longer sentences. "Come on. You're dead on your feet."

"I'm not tired. I have more reading to do, and you said you have work. Right?" Fighting damn hard to keep them open, her eyes rolled.

Fucking adorable. "I do." Fact, if Maggie insisted on staying awake, he preferred her close. Safe. Winter didn't ask again. He took her hand and led them to his office. He'd combined a couple of rooms to accommodate the large stay-at-home sanctuary.

Smiley coralled his thoughts. He was never far away, reminding him of their downtime during a mission, when his friend had his head in a damn book. Swapping paper-backs worked to help them stay sane during the grueling weeks of sun, sand, and shit. His best bud had found it easy to make friends. His laugh acted as a powerful magnet to anyone within earshot. Pity he hadn't heard the RPG and ducked.

"Here okay for you to work, or do you need a desk?" Winter nodded at the leather couch in front of the TV hanging above the fireplace.

"Perfect. I'll start with signing. Let me know if I get too loud." She grinned.

"No problem." Returning her smile, he pulled the throw off the back of the couch and handed it to her. "Keep warm."

"Thanks." She tucked it under her arm, crossed a leg behind her and sat on her foot.

Not sure how she found that comfortable, Winter concen-trated on the map covering his large mahogany desk and did

82

his best to memorize the pattern of red dots. Tactical markers. Finding it hard to focus on anything but Maggie's damn ankle, her toes twisted under her ass. *Shit!* She was a featherweight, but her foot must be numb.

Why not offer to massage her long, slender leg right down to those delicate digits? As if she'd read his mind, Maggie moaned. A throaty groan that had his cock rising to the occasion. "You sure you don't need anything from your room? Laptop? Notebook?"

"Uh-huh. It's all here." She held up her cell and slowly uncurled her leg.

She lifted slightly, allowing her heel to brush against her pussy, and his mouth went dry. "Warm enough?" he croaked and ran his hand across the sweat on the back of his neck.

"Thank you, but you seem tense. Need a massage? I'm amazing at…"

"No. All good, thanks." Afraid he'd say something he wouldn't be proud of, he picked up his pen and glued his gaze on the map.

Finally, around three am, he finished digesting the current intel. Before they landed in Pakistan, he expected changes, but he had a Plan B. Snuffles wafted across the room from the sofa. She had fallen asleep shortly after midnight and he didn't have the heart to wake her.

Soft curves and sweet smells. Her light snoring kept him hard. Twice, he'd almost picked her up and carried her to bed. Instead, he eased the throw out from under her hips and draped it over her slender body.

She mumbled and shifted onto her side, a deep frown creasing the space between her eyebrows. That fucking maniac with the paintball gun had scared her and every one of his protective instincts soared to full alert. First the guy with the forklift and now this. The whole thing smelled fishy.

Winter sat on the floor beside the couch, took hold of Maggie's fingers, and stroked them with the tip of his thumb. To be sure she heard him, he lowered his mouth to her ear and whispered, "Rest. You're safe. Ain't no one getting up those stairs, sweetheart. Sleep."

CHAPTER
THIRTEEN

SEATED NEXT TO HER, Winter had fallen asleep as soon as they boarded the plane that morning. A relief, even if Maggie wished he found her more interesting.

From underneath the short sleeves of the dark T-shirt stretched tight across his defined pecs, his biceps popped. She tried not to giggle but staring at Winter reminded her how her brother had loved the old Popeye cartoon, laughing every time the crazy sailor opened his mouth and swallowed a full can of spinach. Steve had found a hat like the one on the tv show and refused to take it off for an entire summer.

It felt great, comforting, remembering the good times with Steve, but the fact Winter had gone behind her back and complained to Snake still niggled. He'd apologised, but didn't trust her, and she wanted to change that and have him create a better opinion of her. After he saw she could handle herself in Pakistan, she would tell him about Steve and Lazenby's escape.

Storm was going to run into a wall when he ran his extended history check, because once it became clear

Lazenby would keep harassing her, even from prison, she'd changed her name, driver's license, and passport. Professor Ellis knew, and he had been careful wording his recommendation to Snake.

"It's a long flight and I plan to sleep most of it. Suggest you do the same."

Close to the frequency of the plane's engine, Winter's deep baritone rumbled lazily beside her. The vibration made her chest tickle, and she smiled. "I never sleep on planes. Thank heaven for the movies." Maggie tapped the screen on the seat in front of her and brought up the entertainment menu.

"Try. You won't get a chance once we reach Pakistan. Here, use my blanket. I don't need it." Winter shoved his into her lap.

"I'd rather not." Unfortunately, his eyes stayed shut, and he didn't take it back, so she tucked it under her seat. Maggie scratched her forearms, but blanking the image of the countless noses that must have rubbed against it was impossible. Plus, the rough material itched.

"You cold?" Winter asked, peering at her from one half-opened eye.

"A little. The air conditioner is very enthusiastic." Before she could reach up and close the valve, Winter's muscular arm snaked over her head, and he did it for her. The edge of his T-shirt lifted, and boy did he have abs. She guessed at least an eight-pack rippled across his olive skin.

"Better?" he asked.

The man might not trust her, but there was genuine concern in his voice, and she was pretty sure she'd never met anyone as caring as Winter. "Yes, thanks. Sorry to be a pain. Goodnight." Even though it was dark, and they had dimmed the cabin lights, she pulled down the window shade.

There were a hundred options on the entertainment list, and she checked every one of them, trying to find something to watch. Depending on their length, she figured five or six episodes of several TV shows and a couple of movies should see her through to breakfast.

The airline headphones were crap, and her ears were aching before they reached altitude. Thanks to Kenny, she didn't have her good pair. He swore he hadn't taken them, but she knew different.

The screen blurred, and Maggie rolled her lips against the migraine threatening to chew up her eyeballs. Trying not to wake Winter, she did her best not to fidget too much as she dug the Tylenol out of her pocket and undid a bottle of water.

Winter grunted and rubbed the back of his neck. A reflex because he was definitely not awake. Maggie fumbled underneath the seat for his blanket and tucked it over his lower body. Under his chin would be better, but the thin square didn't have a hope in hell of fully covering him.

"I'm fine, Maggie. Drink your water and cover up. It may help you sleep." He crossed his arms and sighed.

"Jeez. How do you do that? Know exactly what I am doing with your eyes closed."

"Practice," he mumbled.

His dark brown voice—yes, voices had color—roared quietly beside her. Like a gentle wave. Now she had her hearing aid again, she heard each one lapping at the shore. Comforting.

Next thing, her whole body vibrated in the darkness surrounding her. The smell of musky male tickled her nose. *Oh hell.* Somewhere in the last twelve hours, she had face-planted Winter's chest.

Maggie reluctantly lifted her head. "Sorry."

"Good to see you finally slept. Breakfast?" Winter tapped her tray table.

She didn't miss the twitch of his lips as she dragged her ear off his shirt. "Want my yogurt?" she asked, deliriously searching for anything normal to say.

"Sure. You're not a fan of passionfruit?"

Oh, hilarious. "No. I don't like the flavor." An understatement. The slimy white sludge made her retch.

"I'll swap you for my OJ." Winter placed the small cup on her tray.

"Thanks. Not a fan?" She winked and wiggled the drink in front of him. Immediately feeling awkward, Maggie wondered if her breath stank. "How long before we land?"

"Just under an…" He turned, and she missed the last bit.

"Sorry, when?" Determined to hear this time, she leaned forward and focused on Winter's mouth.

"An hour." He grinned.

Of course, he'd noticed her gawking. *Arrogant much?* She'd bet every girl who ever met Winter found him irresistible. Before she could park her attention elsewhere, his fingertip brushed her bottom lip.

"Cornflake," he breathed.

Maggie flushed from her toes to the top of her head. "Jesus," she mumbled.

"Sleep well?" His eyes dropped to his shirt.

"Not bad. Usually I can't get comfortable."

"You looked damn cozy to me."

Again, with the breathy growl. Winter's slow gaze skimmed over her breasts, and her nipples pebbled. *Crikey.* When she thought she'd implode from embarrassment, Trigger appeared.

"Morning, you two. I need a word," he said.

For sure, more awake than her. A broad smile softened his craggy features.

"Back soon," Winter grunted.

An obvious afterthought, seeing as he was half out of his seat before he turned to her. But Maggie couldn't pull her gaze from every twitch of his gorgeous lips. Damn infuriating. "Take your time."

"My bad. I should have said. Both of you should be at this briefing. The boss sent pertinent intel you both need to hear," Trigger clarified.

Surprised but glad to be included, she undid her seatbelt and was struggling with her meal tray when Winter leaned over and took it out of her hand.

"Stay. I can catch you up when I get back," he insisted.

Maggie hesitated for less than a second. No way. Trigger had invited her, and she intended to do her job. "No, er, thanks. Look. It's no secret that you aren't happy about me being on this mission, Winter." She sucked in a breath, glad she'd addressed the elephant on the plane, but nervous about how he'd respond. "Everyone from the boss down knows you think I'm incompetent, incapable, in..."

"Indefatigable?" Winter finished with a smirk. She wanted to punch him. "No big deal. I thought you might like to, er, to powder your nose before we land."

And that earned him an eye roll. "I bet. Ms. Messy Face

in the bathroom with her Mickey Mouse toothbrush." Winter gaped at her as she shoved the tray table into place and shuffled out of her seat. Hands planted squarely on her hips, Maggie opened her eyes as wide as possible, willing herself to grow several inches and level with his steely gaze.

"Probably best if she hears the intel first hand," Trigger said, quietly.

"No problem." She inched past Winter. "Follow me, big boy."

"This way." Trigger headed off in the opposite direction.

"Lead on." Winter smirked as she turned and passed him.

Maggie could feel his eyes, red hot lasers boring into her back. "Stop staring at my ass," she swung around and whispered.

"Why? You have a great..."

"Winter..." Trigger warned.

Being angry did horrible things to her insides, turning them to achy mush, but she was this close to losing it with grumble bear. Wasting his time, wondering if she could get the job done instead of focusing on his role. Perhaps he was the liability.

Still rattled when they stopped walking, Maggie looked around for the best place to hear Trigger's briefing. Winter stepped ahead, elbowed one of the other men out of his seat, and nodded for her to sit.

And like that, she couldn't be mad at him anymore. Not for being the sweetest of the four giants surrounding her. Their individual surface mass soared far above average. Large enough to stop any bullets that might come her way. Her stomach somersaulted. Last night's paintballer, crazy kid, was the least of her worries. If Rick Lazenby had found her…

"You, okay?" Winter nudged her elbow.

"Yes." The guy didn't miss a trick.

"Gentlemen, Maggie." Trigger winked at her and began the briefing.

"You sure?" Winter poked, for heaven's sake, the side of her arm.

"Yes, shh." Why wouldn't she be? Like a shower of spring petals, Trigger's English accent calmed her.

"After we left New York, the boss received information that locates Adnan at…" She heard the coordinates, but they didn't mean much. Thankfully, they weren't relying on her for getting them to their destination.

Map reading had never been her forté. No reason to learn, but she nodded and tried to look as though she had a clue.

"There." Winter pointed at the map the guy sitting on his other side had shoved in his hand.

Jeez. Not content to read her mind, he would finish her sentences next.

"After we land in Islamabad at 0400, we will unload and check equipment. At 0600 we head to Adnan's location."

Winter indicated Peshawar. "Oh, he means the place marked in bold, black letters?" Maggie whispered. It took everything in her not to moan.

"To maintain our cover as corporate delegates on our way to the American Business Forum in Lahore," Trigger continued, "a security escort accompanies us as far as Mardan. Storm has our No-Objection Certificates, NOCs. Those, along with our passports and visas, should eliminate potential problems at checkpoints. Maggie, just a reminder, but keep your head covered."

"Will do." She made a mental note to pull her headscarf out of her carry-on before they landed.

"After our escort departs, we press on to Adnan's location. Havoc and I take point. Maggie, you'll remain with Winter, who will provide cover, firepower, if we need it. As soon as we secure Adnan, we will set up an interrogation site. Then it's up to you, Maggie. We're counting on you finding out where he has those nurses stashed. Mission accomplished we return to Islamabad for immediate exfil." Trigger folded his map and scanned their small group. "Questions?"

A ton. But they may not be relevant or appropriate, so she pressed her lips together and straightened her spine. "I won't let you down," Maggie promised. Winter nodded, and a massive wave of relief flooded her entire body. Part of him believed she could do this.

"I know," Trigger added, verbally reassuring her.

They were relying on her, and the weight of that responsibility had the power to bury her. Could she do it? What if Adnan signed in a weird dialect she'd never seen? Her toes curled.

"Maggie," Winter said, his head tilted to one side, a frown on his face.

She wasn't sure how long he had been speaking. Way down the path of failure. She hadn't heard him.

He pointed to the flashing light above her. "Seat belt sign is on. We're landing."

CHAPTER
FOURTEEN

WINTER CRADLED Maggie's shoulders with his fingers, swung her to face him, and made damn sure she had her baby blues fixed on his lips. He had checked earlier to make sure she had her hearing aid, but he wasn't taking any chances. "Take hold of my belt and don't let go. Stay behind me. Not a single eyelash in my peripheral vision. We travel as one. Got it?"

"Yes, sir. Invisible woman at your back. Roger that," she said.

Goddam it. Her cheeky grin never quit. She'd been faking her brave smile ever since they left the airfield.

"Move." Trigger's command rang in Winter's earpiece.

Winter gave Maggie the thumbs up and pushed her firmly behind him. Crouched low, rifle at the ready, heart in his mouth, he advanced. "Moving."

Thank Christ for the predictability of dickhead terrorists. They loved an orderly compound. Men on the right. Women on the left. Close by to service a man's needs from fucking to fighting. Some willing, many not, the females kept one eye on the kids while they hung the washing, the other guarding the perimeter. Often, the first to catch a bullet.

Maggie squeaked and tugged on his belt as he surged forward. Not that he needed any reminder she was there. *Hang on, sweetheart.* They moved together or not at all. Cutting his speed wasn't an option, as he zeroed in on their position by the gate.

Back to the wall, Winter pinned his arm across Maggie's chest. Head on a swivel, he made sure they weren't tracked. On the roof of the building opposite, a single sentry strolled back and forth like it was a summer day in Central Park. Another stood in front of Adnan's quarters, his foot perched on a wooden crate, while he lit a cigarette. *Careless.* No trouble. Winter huffed.

Keeping one shoulder pressed to the wall, he angled toward Maggie. "You holding up?"

"Good." She nodded, but her eyes told a different story. Ever since they'd left Islamabad, he wanted to fuck the mission and put her back on the plane. Get the hell out of there.

"Winter. Come in. Over." Storm's voice echoed in his ear.

"In position. Over," he replied as he gave Maggie's hand a reassuring squeeze. "Wait here."

"No. Don't leave me." Her voice shook.

"S'okay. You'll be safe here. I'll come back for you as soon as I can." Fuck, leaving Maggie was the last thing he wanted to do, but dragging her behind him doubled the chances of them being spotted. Risked all their lives. Most of all, hers.

Still holding her hand, he leaned in and kissed her forehead, his cock jerking against the zipper of his pants at the flash of arousal in her eyes. "Hold that thought," he whispered.

"Go, go, go."

At Storm's command, Winter took off before Maggie changed his mind.

As planned, Trigger and Havoc took point. Storm merged from Winter's left. Heading forward in a well-practiced formation, they zeroed in on their target.

From his position, Winter fired, and the guy hiding behind the empty oil can went down with a what-the-fuck-look on his face. In the distance, a woman screamed and for a second, Winter feared the worst, but a quick glance at the gate confirmed it wasn't Maggie.

Ten seconds later, the small village erupted into a chaotic battleground. Two men burst from the building where they assumed Adnan lived and met the full blast of Havoc's weapon. Taking advantage of the disruption, Winter swept forward, covering Trig's six as he tore ahead. Before the idiots could raise their weapons, Winter had taken care of three more tangos. *Zero points for reflexes, fuckers.*

Storm veered right and peered in the side window. "Target, plus one inside," he confirmed.

"Roger that." Piece of fucking cake. Days like this, Winter wondered why he bothered to show. He should have learned his lesson. Ask Smiley. Out of nowhere, guns firing, three men carrying AK47s burst from the women's quarters. Winter dodged but wasn't fast enough to avoid the sharp sting of a bullet slicing into his arm.

Goddam it. Sweat peppered his brow and blood ran down his arm. Weaving forward, he took out the first guy with a tap to the head. His second bullet blasted a tunnel through the second man's chest. Through the sweat blurring his vision, he clocked Storm run past him and slit the third fucker's throat. Storm never minded getting up close and personal.

Back to back, he fought to stay standing as they spun in a slow circle. Blood from the bullet wound splattered onto his boot. With any luck, it was only a flesh wound. He'd looked death in the eye too many times to bleed out in Pakistan. Besides, he never broke a promise, and Maggie was waiting. Winter bit down hard on the inside of his cheek. *Do not pass the fuck out.*

The door to Adnan's hut gaped open. *Fantastic.* Hazy gray cloaked his vision making it difficult to focus through the sight of his rifle.

"You're hit, man." Storm spat at the dirt.

"Fuck me," Trigger cursed over the comms' static. "Winter?"

"Yeah, yeah. No sweat, but if it's all the same to you, let's hurry this shit up. Maggie's alone, and I'm not in the mood for playing pin-the-tail-on-the-donkey."

Trigger chuckled. "I hear you. On my three. One, two…"

Guns blazing, they advanced. Storm reached the door first and signaled for Winter to cover him as he sailed into Adnan's hut.

"Don't. Move!" Havoc yelled from behind Trigger.

The guy might be deaf, but Adnan sure as hell understood the don't-mess-with-me look burning in his buddy's eyes. Except for a scowl, Adnan hadn't moved a muscle.

Storm checked the man on the ground, making certain he hadn't set off a suicide vest. His head shake earned a collective sigh of relief. Unfortunately, shit-for-brains Adnan snared the moment to locate his cojones and tried to stand. Interesting move, considering Trig had his Glock shoved against the guy's temple. Winter rolled his eyes.

"Sit the fuck down. Unless you want your head blown off," Trigger yelled in the man's ear.

Winter blinked hard several times, determined not to pass the hell out before Maggie was by his side and they were a million miles away from this shit hole.

"Put pressure on the wound." Storm tossed him a rag.

A single chin lift in appreciation was all the thanks he managed. "I look worse than I feel. Story of my life," he mumbled. "I'm going to get Maggie." The room tilted.

"Stop with the superhero shit. I'll fetch her."

Winter would have gone ass over teakettle if Storm hadn't grabbed his arm. "Okay." Not happy, even if it was the smart move. He grabbed the back of a chair and gulped oxygen.

"Mother fucker!" Trigger cursed and smacked Adnan across the face. "Son of a bitch bit me. One more move like that, asshole, and I don't care what the hell you know. You are dead."

Adnan grunted and Winter forced the contents of his stomach back to his belly while Trig grabbed the zip ties from the pocket of his Kevlar and secured fuckhead's hands behind his back. He'd need his fingers when Maggie arrived, but, for now, they were where they belonged.

Howling like a wounded bandicoot, Adnan's spit soared across the room and landed on Winter's boot. As much as he wanted to teach him some manners, Winter maintained his control. But now they had an issue.

"No. Goddamit. Not on my watch. Maggie isn't going

97

anywhere near that fucker," Winter shouted. "One swipe of his hairy ass arm and he'll send her flying into next week."

Slowly, he released his hold on the back of the chair. Squeezing the thing so hard wasn't doing anything to staunch the flow of blood gushing down his arm.

Allowing Maggie within an inch of this guy was insane.

CHAPTER
FIFTEEN

PLASTERED AGAINST THE WALL, hyperaware of her surroundings, not daring to move from the spot where Winter had left her Maggie had never been this hot in her entire life. She glanced at her toes and laughed nervously afraid if she moved, someone might notice and take aim at her shoes.

Impossible, as it was silk, but her scarf felt as though it weighed a ton. As quietly as she could she drew in a breath. She had all but made up her mind to follow Winter and get the interrogation over with when Storm appeared.

"Where's Winter?" The words flew from her mouth, her heart almost beating out of her chest. This wasn't the time to get picky about her escort, but he had promised to come for her.

"Slight hiccup. Nothing to worry about, he's waiting for you. Stay close and I'll take you to him."

They started running and Maggie could tell Storm was taking it easy on her, but she was panting hard by the time they reached Adnan's hut. Next paycheck—a gym membership.

A mattress lay on the floor in the corner, a few once bright rugs covering it. In the other a table and some chairs. One or two were upside down, obviously hit when Trigger and the others had forced entry. Judging by the scattered plates, Adnan had been in the middle of a meal when the guys had burst into his home.

A few crates and what looked like a makeshift stove, made the small room seem overcrowded. Behind a half open curtain, she could make out a toilet and a washbasin.

There wasn't much light, but a Pakistani, she guessed must be Adnan, sat in the chair next to the table. Spitting and yelling, his hands tied behind his back, he scraped his feet in the dirt floor, struggling to stand.

At first, she didn't see Winter in the shadows, leaning awkwardly against a chair. Unease rippled across Maggie's belly when she heard his unmistakable growl, and sharp intake of breath. Blood oozed between the fingers of the hand clamped over his right arm.

"Winter, my God. What happened?" Without waiting for his answer, she flew to his side, and flung her arm around his waist, stroked the back of her hand over his icky gray face. He leaned into her, sighed again before gingerly pulling back his shoulders. Tears welled in her eyes at the moment of vulnerability. "I can't leave you alone for five minutes." The deep lines carving his face softened.

"Don't go all Florence Nightingale on me. It's nothing. If Adnan, the fuckhead, would shut the hell up I'd be fine."

His just-a-scratch attitude didn't fool anyone in the room. The way his neck muscles popped, he had to be in a lot of pain. Maggie had no clue what it felt like to be shot, but men like Winter died before they let anything stop them completing their mission. At least that's what happened in the movies.

Gently pushing her aside, he swayed. *Fine. Have it your way, tough guy.* His raised eyebrow the only sign he'd heard her huff. Sweat trickled down her spine and between her breasts. She brushed her hands over her pants and offered him her own eyebrow comment. *Girl scouts rule.* She pulled a spare scarf from the bag slung across her body and folded it lengthwise. The makeshift bandage would do for now.

CHAPTER
SIXTEEN

WINTER SHRUGGED Maggie's hand from his arm. "Leave it," he snapped. Of all the dumb ass shit to happened. Getting shot when he was supposed to be looking out for her ranked not acceptable. Glassy-eyed, he couldn't figure out if she hated the sight of blood or the fact the situation could endanger them all. "Thanks. I'm good." She bristled at his pathetic stab at an apology.

"Fine but keep pressure on it."

Winter rolled his eyes. Everyone on the goddam planet thought they were a doctor ever since Grey's Anatomy hit the idiot box. Linda had talked about the goddam tv show non-stop during their dinner together.

"You shouldn't be in here. If I have to carry her out of here I will." Starting at Trigger, he staggered as the damn room turned ninety degrees and tossed him on its ass.

"Trig, this is insane." Propped on his good elbow, Winter thumped the side of his head and pleaded with his best friend to see sense.

"I hear you. Life sucks but consider the bigger picture. If

there was another way, don't you think I would take it?" Trigger said in that condescending Brit tone that worked his nerves.

Struggling to get to his feet, Winter pressed his palm against the wall. "How's this for an idea? We transport Adnan to Islamabad and have the Pakistani military interrogate him. That doesn't suit. How's this for a shortcut? I'll waterboard the fucker." He lurched for Adnan who hadn't stopped leering at Maggie. "Eyes on me, motherfucker." Spit flew from his mouth.

Trigger placed his hands on his hips and blew an audible sigh. "Okay, mate. You've still have one good arm, and body language goes a long way. Joking aside, sit you arse down and let Maggie get on with it."

"Please, Winter. How many times must I say it? I can do this," Maggie interrupted.

His best Rambo impersonation didn't faze her, and he was fucking intimidating mid rant, but she took his bellow as a signal to come closer.

"Do as Trigger says, before you fall on your prisoner and this conversation becomes a moot point. If I can't persuade Adnan to tell me anything, Trigger can beat the crap out of him, and you can chuck water over the poor guy until he drowns. Deal?"

Keeping him in the loop, Maggie signed for Adnan who groaned at her threat. *Yeah, dick, that's my woman.* Her courage floored him, melted the icicle fence surrounding his heart. "No," He croaked. The lump in his throat made it hard to speak.

"I vote yes," Trigger said.

"Me too," Storm and Havoc agreed.

"Out-voted, slugger." Trigger's jaw hardened around his final decision.

"Stay by my side." Winter grabbed Maggie's wrist.

"It's okay, Winter. I can walk by myself."

"No argument. Just not in the right fucking direction." He tucked his chin as if frowning at the exit would make her take notice. She dug her heels in and cupped his face.

"I know you're scared, but treating me like an idiot is annoying and unkind."

Bullseye. That last word hit its target. Winter shifted nervously, sheepishly, eyeballing his teammates.

"Everyone has done their job. Now it's my turn." She spoke softly, looking only at him as if the others weren't right there with them. "Snake wanted me on this mission because I'm good at what I do. Do I tell you how to shoot? No. Trust me. I'm sick of arguing and tired. With you here, right beside me, I can do this."

"You better believe it," he mumbled.

"Okay, grizzle-guts." She chuckled. "Fresh start, yes? Let's do this and get you to a hospital."

"Fine." Maggie had talked him into it, but in his head, Winter vowed not to make this the worst decision of his life. "I'll say this, sweetheart. You have enormous balls."

"Impossible. But if you mean anyone would need a pair to face Adnan, I'll take it as a compliment." She winked. "Now sit there, next to me." She pointed at the chair he'd clung to earlier. "Save your strength in case we need it."

One look at Maggie's slim body, and a person might believe the first sign of trouble would blow her away, but down low in his gut, Winter suspected they'd only scraped the surface of her strength.

"Come here." He was hungry for a taste of her courage and terrified of what might happen in the next ten minutes, so he threw his good arm around her shoulders, hugged her close, and lost himself in the blue of her eyes. The tip of her tongue swept across her bottom lip, and his cock stirred. When this shit was over, he and Maggie King were going to have a long talk.

The breeze drifting through the open door played with the fine hair caressing her shoulders. Stuck to her like glue, he wouldn't hesitate to make good on his promise and carry her the hell out of there.

"You have ten minutes to secure the intel we need. No argument when I call time. Got it?"

"Got it!" The rest of his team chimed in.

"Yes." She smiled her answer and Winter wondered how Maggie King kissed.

CHAPTER
SEVENTEEN

WINTER MUST HAVE HEARD her heart thundering in her chest.

"You good?" he asked.

Maggie curled her fingers into tight fists and thanked the stars he was with her. "Yes." Afraid to say more in case she reneged, she dropped her shoulders, but the tension headache building behind her eyeballs wouldn't quit. Signing in Adnan's Pashto dialect—no problem. Understanding him if he raised his chin off his chest and signed actual sentences—tick.

It was one thing to say, I can do this, but she knew nothing about interrogating a terrorist. A knife edge to her skills. Slowly inhaling, she tried to focus on Winter and his team, all the terrified people in nearby villages desperate to live a normal life without constant threat.

If the kidnapped nurses weren't dead, who knew what state they'd be in when they found them? If they found them. Earlier sounds of gunfire, women screaming, children running for their lives, collided in her head. Gulping air, she thumped her ears, trying to block out the memory—the noise.

"Enough," Winter croaked. "Havoc. Get her out of here."

Maggie sure as heck wished she could leave, run far and fast from the ugly place, but the pain in Winter's black eyes, his concern, hit her with the force of a tornado. Her warrior was hurting. Stuck in this crazy hell hole, she wanted to stop herself from flinging her arms around his neck, hugging him, swearing she was in control. "No."

"You sure?" He shook his head. "Say the word and…"

"I've got this," Maggie repeated. Stronger this time, hoping he'd believe her. Trust her more than she did herself. Reluctantly, she left the safety of Winter's gaze and returned her attention to Adnan.

"Please untie him."

Winter grunted, but she turned to Storm. His eyes narrowed, as happy about doing what she asked as Big Bear, but he slashed the rope with his knife. "Thank you."

Not knowing how else to confirm her neutrality, she held out her hand to Adnan.

Immediately, Winter caught her wrist and shook his head. "No touching."

She nodded and took a step back. "Hello. My name is Maggie. Calm down. Let's talk," she signed.

Adnan's hands flew in wide, mostly inarticulate gestures. But one sentence came through loud and clear. "They have my children," he bellowed.

"Shut the fuck up."

Winter kicked Adnan's foot, but the man's anguish was genuine, plain as the bugs circling the ceiling above his head. Ready to scream, too Maggie swallowed the bile pooling in the back of her throat. *Pull it together!* There was more at stake here than her queasy tummy, and time was fast running out for the kidnapped nurses.

"What's he saying?" Trigger asked, a forced calm in his tone.

"That he won't talk. If he does, they will kill his children."

Trigger stepped forward. "And if they don't, you can bet your life I will. Talk," he growled and raised his fist.

"No. Don't." Certain he meant to hit Adnan, she stepped between them.

Winter's roar echoed off the stone walls as he sprang to his feet, the chair falling behind him. Despite his injury, he lifted her off the ground and swung her to his opposite side. "Crazy woman. What the hell?"

The sudden move had taken away her breath. Unable to speak, she wiggled out of Winter's grasp and thrust her chin roughly into the air and cried out at the sudden crick in her neck.

"Enough." Winter didn't shout, but the bitter tone made his intention clear.

Desperately trying to figure out what she should do next, Maggie's eyes darted from Winter to Trigger and back to Adnan. "Okay, okay. Dumb move. It won't happen again. Please. Let me try."

Trigger nodded. Shakily, she dodged Winter and glared at Adnan. His cheeks were hollow, his eyes sunk deep behind bushy eyebrows. Tears streamed down his face. Thin, under his cotton kameez, he didn't look scary, he looked in need of a decent meal.

"Are you hungry?" The question, as good a place to start

as any. She shot Winter a quick look, nodding at the wall beyond his shoulder, and hoped he'd take the hint and step away. Give her space. Reaching for the canteen of water on the table, she held it to Adnan's lips.

"Maggie," Winter warned.

She ignored him. After all what could Adnan do with Trigger's gun pointed at his head? She let go of the canteen and signed. *"Drink. You must be thirsty."*

Once again, her stupidity cost her. Most of his spit missed, but the flash in the corner of her eye was all the warning she had before Winter grabbed Adnan's throat. A loud crack splintered the air, forcing their captive's head to jerk at an odd angle. When Winter raised his arm to strike him again, she blocked his aim, and the blow ricocheted through her bones.

"Stop, Winter. If you beat him to death, he can't tell us anything." She didn't know the rules of this dick swinging game, only that if she backed off now, she would lose big time. Dropping her shoulders away from her ears, she shoved one foot forward and glared at him. "Leave. If you can't handle it."

Maggie held her breath, expecting, any second, Winter would carry out his threat and haul her out of the hut. His fists dropped to his side, but his anger and something she could swear looked like fear bubbled in his black eyes. When she thought he'd explode, he blinked, and the chaos building between them calmed. Because it wasn't fear. Something much more mind-blowing and complicated spun between them, making them vulnerable and unsure.

They wanted the same thing, to know where Adnan had hidden the nurses, but they had very different ideas on how to get there, and in a short time, she'd begun to care, spent an unreasonable amount of time concerned with what Winter thought about her, felt for her. From the bizarre combination of rage and concern written all over his grumpy face, she suspected something similar messed with his head.

Instead of arguing, she reached for his hand. Immediately he pulled away, boundary, distance, but she refused to let him get away with it. She tried again, and this time, he allowed her to uncurl his fingers. "You can be mad at me later." And I'll show you how we'll make up, she thought, but didn't say, because it would take a lot longer than the next few hours for their hearts to act human. "I will take care of Adnan while Storm patches you up, because I am counting on you to get me out of here."

CHAPTER
EIGHTEEN

WINTER STRADDLED the burned-out oil drum outside Adnan's, supporting his weight on the hand pressing heavily on his bent knee, while Storm checked Maggie's scarf. He drew the line at the sling their self-appointed medic wrangled from his pack.

"Why is she taking so fucking long?" His voice was weak, rough, unlike the power of his boot stamping the dirt. More like a tired child denying bedtime.

"When it's done, it's done."

The condescending platitude made it out of his Storm's mouth the same time Maggie stumbled from the hut. His lip curled at the sight of Trigger's arm supporting her waist. She'd been right to throw him the fuck out.

He'd been close to destroying the entire mission because he couldn't keep his alpha dick in check. Hands down, he was the sorriest of the pair, but Maggie wasn't breathing deep enough so anyone would notice. Dead on her feet, she stumbled straight to him.

"Feeling better? Storm's done a good job with patching you up," she said, checking the knot in her scarf.

Shaky voice. Tears in her eyes. No bruises or marks he could see. His teammates had taken care of her. The burn in his arm made him cross-eyed, but he had to be sure. He swayed to his feet and held out his hand, hoping she'd take it, give him the skin on skin contact he craved.

"Our terp did good." Trig nodded. Admiration stamped clearly on his face.

Did he ever really doubt that would be the case? "What now?"

"Havoc's getting Adnan ready to travel. Snake's aware of the hostage location and the London team is on their way. Our orders are to hand our friend in there over to the authorities in Islamabad before we hop on our plane home. That suit?"

Cocky much? Winter ignored the sarcasm. Frankly, he was in too much pain to take the son-of-a-b on right now. Shaky on his feet, Storm moved to catch him, but Maggie beat him to it, wrapping her arms around him and holding him tight.

Taking it as a sign she might forgive him for being such a dick, he faked a moan, gave her some of his weight and skimmed his nose over the top of her head. Did she smell of roses? Nah, only in the movies given the heat and dust, but he closed his eyes and inhaled. Whispered thanks to Senora Ortega's god that Maggie was safe, tucked against him where she belonged.

"Okay Doc." Trigger winked. "Let's give Havoc a hand to bring round the vehicle."

"We need a man for each wheel?" Storm shrugged. Trig raised his boot to his ass. "Oh."

Silently, Winter thanked his teammates for pushing off and giving him and Maggie space.

"He didn't touch you?" He lifted her chin, so she had to look him in the eyes. No room for any of her fake it-'til-you-make-it lies.

"No. I could sleep for a week, but I'm okay. It's you I'm worried about. There's an awful lot of blood on your shirt."

The light kiss she planted on his stubble floored him. "Maggie, I..."

"Shh. It's just a thank you kiss."

"Not *just* a kiss, sweetheart. I should never have doubted you. I'm so damn proud. We couldn't have done this without you." He nuzzled the top of her head, a chill running through him at what he said next. "This is killing me, but this can't happen."

"Wow, Winter. A full sentence when two words would have done the job. Not interested, that's all you had to say." She shrugged but kept her gaze fixed on his. "Whatever. No problem."

"It is for me." Maggie had her pride, and why would an old, battle worn dickhead like him be anyone special? "Kissing you when we're riding an adrenaline spike. It isn't right letting you do something you may regret later." He could be making shit worse, giving mixed messages, but she looked lost, so he cupped her head and pressed her against his Kevlar. The spot above his heart.

Maggie lifted her foot and stomped on his toe. Taking advantage of her surprise attack, she slipped out of his arms. "You need help to get to the truck?"

Pity her feet hadn't shifted an inch. Damn, but he smiled.

"Don't," she half whispered, a tear rolling down her cheek.

Ask him to prevent a military coup, take down hostile insurgents, no problem. Find words, the perfect move to stop a woman crying, and he froze.

"Hell, Winter. Say something."

"Why? When for all my adult intentions, I'd much rather do this." He leaned in, close enough to blow gently across her lips.

A weak fist thumped his chest. Christ, he loved her pouty mouth. Maggie King lit him up, like fireworks on the fourth of July. He angled his head and pressed his forehead against hers, ran the tip of his tongue along the seam along her lips. So sweet. A throaty groan vibrated in his chest.

"Open your mouth. Wider." Palming the back of her neck, he pleaded for a kiss certain to blow his ever-loving mind.

Greedy fingers grappled with his Kevlar, and smooth as soft serve ice-cream her tongue slipped inside his mouth and swept in a claiming circle. Another part of his anatomy throbbed, and he almost forgot about his injured arm.

Clasping her upper arms pulled her away as gently as he could. "You must know what I'd love to do with you right now, but it can't happen. Not here. Not now."

Maggie winced.

"Fuck me if I haven't wanted to kiss you senseless ever since you disappeared with my jacket." He held onto her a fraction longer than he should. If his heart stopped beating before his next inhale, it would be exactly what he deserved. Many times, in the dead of night, when his nightmares refused to quit, he'd prayed for it to do just that, begged.

Not today. The memory of Maggie's mouth on his drove him wild. His cock pressed urgently against his zipper, pushing, vowing life could only get better if he took her to bed.

Mind off your dick. Roger that. Pointless, wishing for stuff to be normal, so he forced his hands to his sides. Too young, and he guessed inexperienced, to appreciate his kind of bedroom fun. Maggie deserved more than a fucked-up cynic. In a few years, happily married with kids, she'd thank him for curbing his overactive libido.

Winter caught her tear on the side of his thumb and came close to pissing off the good guy inside him and ignoring the fact they had to work together. A one-night stand didn't belong in the same sentence as her. Didn't fucking exist. If he did this, eventually, not tomorrow or next week, but ultimately, he would hurt her. No picket fences on his horizon. No fluffy kittens or boutique crossbreeds. Numero uno, no kids.

More than a decade older, he had a serious case of super-hero protector. Nothing else. Proof? The hand that had snuck to hover over the small of her back, near enough to feel her warmth caress his palm before her cute ass stomped to their vehicle.

Mistake, he mumbled under his breath and dragged his eyes above her waist. Her slow, satisfied grin stared back at him. Spellbound since that day on the pier when he had clocked her blonde hair fleeing from her beanie. Maggie King owned him.

CHAPTER
NINETEEN

WHY DO I BOTHER! Nothing fucking works out for me. No matter how much time I spend working shit out, planning the perfect moment.

Okay, I admit it. I was slow, shouldn't have waited, got my ass moving sooner and grabbed her when I had the chance.

The rain was awesome. And me, sitting in the car, heater turned up, wiping the steam off the window, just so I wouldn't miss a single minute of her terror as she tried to sleep a second night in that park.

Shadows jumped, and the wind howled like one of those horror movies. "Boo!" Laugh. I ask you. Having fun. An unrealistic expectation? But after being locked up in that shithole, I deserved a treat. Five fucking years of my life, that bitch stole from me.

Then that ape showed up and snatched Maggie King right out of my hands. I followed them. Prepared to take big boy on and finish this shit, I go out of the car, made it onto the sidewalk. Then abracadabra, the paintballer appeared out of nowhere.

Mother fucker. Epic. Almost soiled my jocks when he zapped her in the chest and red paint spread across her tits.

Now that I think about it, returning to the car, drinking myself to sleep that night was my bad. Sloppy. 'Cause the next day, poof. She'd vanished.

Took me two days before I fronted that hooker at Sentinel. Ready to oblige, carved into the ton of make-up on her face. She couldn't wait to give me what I wanted. Thought it fan-fucking-tastic when I said I was her brother, in town for a few days, looking to take sis to lunch.

Now I'm holed up in this shithole of a motel, waiting for her to get back from Pakistan! Can't imagine she's having any fun there. Soon. Maggie King. Soon.

CHAPTER
TWENTY

TWO WEEKS since they had returned to New York and time had zipped along—no sign of Lazenby. Maggie wanted to believe Esposito when he claimed Steve's killer had skipped the country, but she didn't. Luck like that never came her way. His escape, knowing the cops hadn't caught him, mashed all of Maggie's fears together and hurled them into every minute of her day.

It was only a matter of time.

All morning, including the extra ten minutes in Winter's super shower, she kept telling herself to relax and enjoy her first day alone, since they got back from Pakistan. Out with the girls. Sam had arranged it and was outside waiting for her. "Thanks for giving me a ride. I could have caught the subway."

Arms folded loosely across her body, Snake's wife leaned against her car. Dressed in jeans and a pale blue shirt, she looked as relaxed as Maggie hoped to feel one day.

"Winter would have a fit if I let that happen. Snake is

semi-trained, but when we first arrived in the Big Apple, you would think we'd landed on a post-apocalyptic planet inhabited by flesh-eating monsters, and I didn't know how to shoot and leave some other bunny to ask questions later." Sam pointed to the passenger side. "Come on. Where is Winter? I half-expected him to join our girl time."

"I threatened to tie him to the sofa if he didn't rest."

Sam wriggled her eyebrows. "Maggie. Woman of many surprises. Love the idea of the alpha dog in ropes."

"Oh, no, nothing like that." Maggie blushed. After their kinda kiss, he'd backed off completely. Disappointing. Her mom said girls didn't chase boys, but heeding her advice was difficult. Many times, she had considered jumping Winter's bones and pulled back at the last minute. Shyness had never been her problem before Lazenby destroyed her family. Life had breezed on by while she hung out in her past.

Sam got it right. Since the mad paintball incident, Winter didn't let her go anywhere without him. According to him, joining Sentinel meant more than a job. They were a family.

Deep down, she wanted to believe him. Family, like she used to have, where people were honest with their feelings and loved you no matter what. A place where the rough and smooth deserved love and support.

Life was never the same after mom and dad lost their son. They died in a car accident a year after his death. Sometimes, usually at two am when she couldn't sleep, she tortured herself, believed she must have done something wrong.

Sam stared at her, watching as she drifted away. Maggie

grabbed the door handle, "Winter's reading," she added as they piled into the car.

"Seriously. Winter reading? We are talking about the same alpha bear? The latest ball game stats?" Sam grinned and checked her side mirrors.

"Go ahead, poke fun, but I lent him my favourite book of Jacques Prevért's poems."

"*Paroles*, right? I remember those from school. They're in French." Sam chuckled. "Duh, of course they are."

They both laughed, Sam's eyes widening to the size of a plasma tv screen. "Uh-huh. I handed him a beer and a sandwich and left him a dictionary. That should keep him busy."

"Champion. Because we have a big day. Jenna is meeting us at the yarn shop. You haven't met her yet. She's the company's in-house medic. Another Brit and an old friend. I'm lucky. She and her son, Tom, came with us when we moved. Linda will be there, too."

"Oh." Stupidly, she hadn't realized she was joining them. Although, she had called every day, insisting to speak to Winter.

Sam frowned. "Is that a problem?"

"No. Great," Maggie quickly added, shoving aside the spark of mean in her tone. "Girl power." She raised a weak fist in the air. "I'm looking forward to meeting your friend. Was Jenna in the military too?"

"God, no. Too busy putting herself through med school and raising a grumpy teenager. You know, iPad is god with a capital G, and I only change my socks once a week stage."

Maggie laughed. Sam's open and friendly manner, along with her creative cussing at the crazy traffic on the Brooklyn

Bridge, worked wonders at easing the tension of the past few weeks. Shifting to her right, she ducked her head to get a better view through the rails at Manhattan. Awesome.

Her folks had brought them to the city during school holidays, but the skyline had changed since she was a kid. She and Steve would argue over which was tallest, the Empire State building or the Chrysler building. Today, heavy gray clouds swallowed the peaks of new high-rise developments.

Maggie strained her neck eager to glimpse at One World Trade Center. Now the tallest skyscraper and the site of the 911 Memorial. She remembered her dad praising the men who had joined the military shortly after the twin towers fell. Half expecting to find Winter sitting in the back seat, she turned to check.

"Oh, for Pete's sake, knob head." Sam smacked the horn at the yellow cab up ahead, darting across lanes. "I have no idea what this heavy-footed muppet arse thinks he's doing. Speeding to the next red light?"

Maggie shrugged. New York cabbies were pushy, but from what she'd heard, no worse than taxi drivers in London.

"Well done, plonker," Sam yelled at the guy who was now five cars ahead, tailgating a black SUV.

Thanks to downtown traffic being twice as bad as on the Bridge, by the time they'd handed the car over to the valet at the parking garage, they had to sprint the couple of blocks to the yarn store.

"Oh, shit!" Sam nodded toward Linda standing outside the shop, tapping her foot.

"You're late," she grumbled.

The woman had nerve getting mad at the boss' wife. "Sorry," Maggie blurted. "I wasn't ready when Sam arrived. Hope you haven't been waiting long?"

Sam pushed past a huffing Linda and opened the door. "You are going to love this store, Maggie."

"'Scuse me." Maggie tried to follow, turning sideways to squeeze past the self-appointed guard who glared at her. "Do you knit?" she asked, to be friendly.

"No," Linda walked inside to look at a rack of knitted sweaters in the corner.

Then why the heck have you bothered to come? Maggie opened her mouth to apologize again for taking up everyone's time, but Sam interrupted, returning with another woman.

"Maggie, Linda. This is Jenna. She was away for Snake's recent recruitment drive, but I'm happy to report that the female side of Sentinel is growing."

"Hi, I'm Maggie. Pleasure to meet you." Especially as Jenna was holding a huge ball of gorgeousness. A thick green yarn that matched the color of her kind, friendly eyes. Same bewitching shade as her friend Josie's eyes. Guys surrounded them the minute they hit the bar that horrible night. With her long auburn hair flowing over her shoulders, she'd held court while the drinks kept coming.

"Hi. And the pleasure is all mine. Sam says you suggested this place. Excellent choice. It took me all of two minutes to find this ball of lovely."

"Glad you like it. I can't wait to catch up."

"Go ahead. I'm off to find some buttons for Snake's shirt. About time he realized I'm not just a pretty face," Sam said.

Maggie headed over to the wall overflowing with the most amazing colors and textures she had ever seen. A glance at the door confirmed Linda's face hadn't changed. If anything, the frown between her eyebrows was deeper.

Just her luck. The skein of yarn she'd been eyeballing from the moment she set foot in the store lived on the highest rack by the window. As she passed Linda, she smiled, but didn't stop to talk. She stood on the small, conveniently placed, stool and peered over the top shelf.

No! Maggie gasped. She could swear it was Lazenby across the street, staring at the store. A van drove past, and he vanished, swallowed by the crowd scuttling along the street. Stupidly, she stepped back, recoiling from the threat, and slipped off the step.

"Steady, woman." Sam grabbed her elbow in time to stop her from falling and making a complete idiot of herself. "Knocked out by the brightness of that yarn?" she teased.

"Something like that." Heart thudding in her ears, Maggie clutched the fluro pink skein of merino. "I thought I saw someone I knew," she lied, forcing a smile, mainly because she didn't want a fuss and it had to be a mistake, but a call to Detective Esposito when she got home couldn't hurt.

"Are we done?" Linda tossed her question from the doorway. "Probably your brother. We're starving. Right, Jenna?"

"Guess so." Looking sheepish, Jenna nodded. "You got what you need, Maggie?"

Brother? She must have misheard Linda. Now she had some free time, she'd make an appointment at the clinic and check her new hearing aid was working okay. Suddenly, the guilts hit. After all, they were supposed to be going to lunch.

"Yes, sorry, all done. Let me pay for this." A quick check out the window confirmed no Lazenby in sight. Her imagination gone wild. She hurried to the counter.

Linda grunted and opened the door, the tiny bell above her head jangled. *Linda has left the building.*

CHAPTER
TWENTY-ONE

NOT KNOWING which way to turn, Maggie stared at Winter's front door. Loaded to the max with food shopping she nodded at Senora Ortega. Winter's neighbor waved and bent to poopy scoop after Chula, her Maltese Shih-tz something or other. They both smiled at her twirling on the top step like a ballerina in lead boots.

If acting smart had been on today's must-do list, she would have made sure she had a finger free to punch in the security code. One wrong move and she risked losing the bags hanging like dead weights from her shoulders.

Donkeys go better loaded. Her mother's cheery complaint niggled in her ear. Before today, she'd never understood what she meant. All those Saturdays Mom had walked blocks with the family grocery shopping because she refused to pay a cab to take her from A to B.

It had been three weeks since they returned from Pakistan, and Jenna was ready to sign Winter off with a clean bill of health. More than fine with taking care of himself, he hadn't really needed her help, but insisted she stay with him until she rented her own apartment.

Suited Maggie. Sleeping on the streets was great, said no one ever, and if Lazenby found her, she had no actual skills to protect herself. Having a permit, but no gun, meant she never wasted energy wondering if she could shoot anyone.

The gunshot wound to Winter's arm wasn't life threatening, but Snake insisted he take the time off to heal, and she was more than glad to help. Unfortunately, rest didn't come easy to the big bear. The day he woke up insisting on putting in a new back door so she wouldn't be attacked by unwanted visitors while she took a shower, she lost it and had to wrestle the hammer from his hand. Winter's pacing drove her nuts.

The only way she could get him to take a nap was if she read to him. Yep, turned out the five-year-old living in his giant body loved a bedtime story.

Used to getting his own way, he had developed selective deafness whenever she suggested he use his down time to scan the internet and help her find an apartment. Sadly, they hadn't even cuddled since their FUBAR of a kiss. There must be a way to convince Winter to try again. Or she'd die trying.

"Need help?" Winter's deep voice rumbled over the intercom.

Maggie jumped. "Where are you? You are still supposed to be resting." Impossible idiot. She looked up at the security camera, half-expecting two beady eyes to be staring back at her.

"On the couch, like you ordered."

"I bet you are," she said, rolling her eyes for the benefit of

Senora Ortega who had switched her attention from cleaning up after Chula to the soap opera rocking it on the stairs.

"Hope you bought Pringles," Winter said.

Maggie smiled at the chuckle in his voice. Then she remembered that a man his size could eat an entire canister by himself, and she'd only grabbed one. Ranch flavor—Winter's favorite. *Go back and grab the cheesy kind.*

"Sure you don't want any help? First and last chance," he offered, his voice drooling with amusement.

"I'm fine." She leaned closer to the intercom. "And when I reach your office, mister, you better be flat on your back."

Winter and Senora Ortega both cleared their throats. "Lying in front of the TV, watching the game," Maggie said with a groan.

At the bottom of the stairs, Senora Ortega's dog had sufficiently marked his territory and yipped.

"Looks like the park is calling my honey. Have a nice day." She waved and headed toward the pier.

"You too." Maggie sighed. How great would it be to stay in New York? Get a dog? But with no firm leads on Lazenby, she had no idea what he'd do next. He must be the paint-baller. A crazy threat to make sure she understood he was close. Able to get to her anytime he wanted.

On edge, she had been looking over her shoulder ever since she left Food Bazaar. Winter hadn't wanted her to go alone, insisting that the five-minute walk was too long for her to be out of his sight. To prove it, he'd sent her five text messages in ten minutes demanding an update on her ETA. But as much as she loved spending time with Winter, she couldn't stay cooped up forever.

Raising her shoulder she jammed one bag in the crook of

her, sucked in her gut, and leaned forward to punch the security pad. Unfortunately, the string number had snagged the railing. A sharp yank set it free, but momentum took over, sending her, eggs, and Winter's Pringles torpedoing forward as the front door swung open. She gasped, grateful for the large, very welcome hand that caught her before she collided with the top step.

With a grunt, she straightened quickly, marched past him, and headed up the stairs. "Coming?" she yelled, placing the shopping on the floor at the top. When he didn't answer, she turned and caught him standing inside the doorway where she'd left him, admiring her ass. "Oh, you are so busted." Secretly glad Winter was showing interest, she twirled her hips in a slow circle.

Winter's lips quirked a fraction of a second before he bounded up the twenty steep stairs two at a time, a predatory glint in his honey-brown eyes. "No!" she yelped and flew to his office, making it to his couch as he sailed through the door. "Lie down," she commanded. Unable to ban the laughter in her voice, she spread her legs wide and pointed at the piece of furniture.

"Yes, sir, ma'am. How do you want me? Hands above my head or behind my back?"

Damn those dimples. Christ, he was gorgeous. "Don't tease Winter. I might be tempted to tie you up. Helpless, who knows what I could do to you?"

"Now, that's where I can help. How about you…"

She was having a hard time keeping her distance. The low flutter in her belly pushing her to ask why he'd finally stopped denying the obvious physical attraction and take whatever was going on between them to the next level?

Christ, she hoped so, because there couldn't be a better plan in the world than taking the scarf from around her neck, handing it over, and telling him to show her every trick in his wicked little book. "Iced tea, that's what you need." Maggie wiggled her eyebrows. Not very sophisticated. Hopefully, a clear signal she wanted to play.

"But it's forty degrees outside," he moaned with a wink.

Adorable. "Not so you would notice." She fanned her face.

"Come here." Winter crooked his index finger.

Heaven on a stick. The man must realize what he did to her girly bits. "Pity you're on drugs. I'm of a mind to pour me a mighty long beer."

"Not so fast." Before she could brush past him, Winter's hands were on her hips, tugging her closer. "I'm going to kiss you, Maggie King. Any objections?

"None. I'm not the one who put the brakes on in Pakistan." The smile fell from his face and his eyes turned black. *Wow!* If she'd messed this up, she'd scream. She ground into the hardness pressing against her pelvis, not knowing why a single blink from Winter made her contemplate doing things with him she'd only read about in girly magazines. "Forget I said that. Honestly, yes." Desperately trying to catch the breath skipping away with her, she gulped. "Please. I really want you to ki—"

"Good. Stop talking. Hold still."

The tip of Winter's tongue nudged the corners of her lips, robbed her of breath. A tickle shot straight to her clit. *Oh. My...* His mouth plundered hers, claiming her permission to enter. Why now, what had changed? Who cared? Keeping her eyes closed, she hummed approval at his tongue sweeping the inside of her mouth.

"Bedroom," he growled.

"I get you're a man of few words, but how about, please?" She pressed her whole body hard against him, loving the need shining in his eyes.

"Triple please." His head tilted to one side. "I plan on being in credit."

"I should put away the groceries," she croaked. Hardly surprising she couldn't hide the giggle in her groan.

"Fuck the groceries."

"Jesus, Winter. I hate you."

"Yeah? Your body disagrees."

He tweaked her right nipple hard enough to make her toes curl before scooping her into his massive arms, flopping onto the couch, and pulling her into his lap. Which would have been hilarious if he wasn't injured. None of this was funny when she allowed reason to push forward. Especially his sudden change of mind. What happened to, *we can't do this?* "Let me go. Please."

"Sure." Winter immediately dropped his arms, allowing her to stand.

She needed space to think, to sort out the confusion that refused to stop messing with her brain. "I have to pee." That should kill his arousal. "And you should rest. You're still under doctor's orders."

Day-old stubble shadowed his chin. Lethal, she reminded herself. She headed for the bathroom before she climbed right back into Winter's arms and lost herself in his amazing brown eyes, jet black with arousal.

CHAPTER
TWENTY-TWO

STAY RIGHT WHERE YOU ARE. Blaming Maggie's swift change of mind on his mixed signals, Winter pressed his palms into his thighs. Once he'd made up his mind, switching positions wasn't his style. Until the whirlwind that was Maggie King shook his world.

He meant every word he'd said in Pakistan. He was too old. They worked together. God help him, he'd tried. If he'd taken Sam up on her offer and let Maggie stay with them, things could have been different. Out of sight, getting a grip on his arousal, regaining control easier.

Yeah, nah. More than wanting to take her to bed, he fucking loved her company. When she was around, the smile on his face kept right on coming. Knowing she slept in the room opposite him, he woke every morning with a satisfied grin heaving on his cheekbones. Any accidental brush of her hand made him hard. The shy, roving glances she took when she thought he wasn't looking.

But more, at the top of the list of reasons to keep her close, sat protecting her very sexy ass. Maggie didn't think he knew about what happened the other day, but concerned for her safety, Sam had told him about their possible stalker. No smoke without a fucking fire, grandfather used to say. *Damn right.*

His pulse hammered against his temples. He clocked six more beats before he surrendered, admitted he wanted Maggie King more than his next breath. Finally done with his half-assed excuses.

They worked together but offering that up as his reason not to take the risk didn't hold. Take Snake and Havoc and their partners. Like them, Winter had a sneaky suspicion once he made love to Maggie, once wouldn't be enough.

Beyond the age difference, nothing would turn him on more than seeing Maggie come apart in his arms, but he took women to his bed who shared his need to love hard. If he scared her, hurt her in any way, he'd slit his fucking wrists. *Take it slow.* Any which way, they should talk.

"Hey, wait up." Before he convinced himself not to, he surged to his feet and caught her at the bottom of the stairs. Cupping the back of her neck in one hand, he grabbed her hand with the other and drew her to him.

"You are fucking irresistible," he groaned into the smooth silky skin below her ear.

Miserably failing to keep his distance, control his lust for the delectable angel, he kissed her. Breathed into her soft mouth words that had no voice, drank her soft cries as she shuddered against him. Panting like the dog he was, he switched his hand from hers, clasped her ass and lifted her off her feet. "Legs around my waist."

"Okay, okay." She laughed.

As fast as he dared, pinned between Maggie's legs, he

raced them to his bedroom. Mid-air, he flipped onto his back to brace her fall when they landed. "As much as I enjoy your laugh, sweetheart, give me back your damn mouth."

Kisses whispered across the bridge of his nose. Christ, he'd been lucky to bed many fine-looking women, but none came close to this beauty. The delicate light that surrounded her seared through the mountain of shit burying his soul.

Stroke for stroke, their tongues tangled in, out, up, down, and around. If life ended now, he'd beg to go another round to die in her arms. Thrusting his knee between her legs, he separated her thighs and rubbed against her sex.

Her soft moans hardened his arousal to the point of blissful fucking torture. She dived for the flesh below his ear, tormenting him with nips and licks that made his blood boil. Wet and warm, her mouth traced the thick column of his neck, raced across his chest and sucked his nipple through the rough denim of his shirt.

"Jesus." They were fully clothed, but if Maggie kept working him like this, he would come before she did. And that could not happen. Her first, falling apart in his arms, at least once, before he slipped inside her. One hand cradling her skull, the other holding her delicate body, he rolled her under him. Careful to keep his weight on his elbows so he didn't crush her, he lost himself in her smiling blue eyes.

"Wow," she panted.

No argument. "Have you any idea what I want to do to you?" Winter stroked a strand of hair from the side of her mouth.

"Seriously, Winter? I would have to be asleep. And I'm not sure even that would work." Her hand slipped between them and stroked his cock.

"Mmm. So we're clear." He swept his tongue over the pulse point on her neck. "I mean to taste every fucking inch of you before I lose myself in your wet heat."

"Promise?" she whispered and gave him a squeeze that made his eyes cross.

"Too many clothes," he growled as his blood pressure spiked past humanly possible and kept on truckin'.

She's not for you. As hard as he struggled to keep that reality from messing shit up, his earlier concerns raised the big guns, refusing to take a hike. All his life, he swore never to fall deep for any woman. Not in his line of work. No guarantees. No certainty he'd return from a mission. Ask Smiley's woman how it felt to get the knock on the door. To hear your soul mate wasn't coming home. Wife, kids? He couldn't do that to them.

Sentinel was all the family he needed, but hell he wanted Maggie King beside him for more than a night. Who the fuck knew what turned him on the most, her hot mouth or the warm damp of her sex writhing against his thigh? It didn't matter. They were a killer combination.

Add sexy and smart and he was a goner. Way ahead of him, his cock ached to be balls-deep inside her, until all his doubts slid into home base with the force of a nuclear rocket.

"We. Can't. Do. This." The strangled words broke free, dragging with them a shit ton of guilt.

"Oh." Maggie yelped.

There was no force behind her fist punching his chest, but the blow shook him to his boots. Eyes shut, blocking him, Maggie rolled out from under him and landed on the floor.

"Easy. Let me explain." He held out his hand, offering to

help her up, but she was having none of it. Could he blame her? Head high, she scrambled to her feet and glued her arms to her body. Words floated like stunned fish inside his head. And in the end, "Sorry," was all he could fucking offer.

"You are pathetic."

Unlike his voice, Maggie's stayed steady. She stormed out of his room, slamming the door behind her before he could rattle off any feeble explanation.

Pathetic. She got that right. Driven by his raging hard on, he had broken his golden rule, and hurt her. Ego talking. A woman as together as Maggie didn't need him. Winter hung his head and pounded his ears with his fists. Things could be different if he moved out of his own messed up way.

Let her go. Read a goddam book. That worked for about fifteen minutes before his feet were skating after her. Maggie sat on the edge of her bed. Pale, tight lipped. He hovered in the doorway and waited for her to tear him a new one. Anything had to be better than her nowhere stare. Her silence shredded what time had left of his heart.

Three steps, and he could hear her breath. Two more and he would bring her into his arms. Another, before he stretched her out and claimed her. He kneeled in front of her. "That should never have happened."

"You got that right." Maggie shrugged and stared at the floor. "But no sweat, Winter. I understand."

His breath hitched with a warning. *Don't speak.* Maggie could never be his. He closed his eyes and swallowed the massive lump in his throat. "You're too young. Too good," he rasped.

Maggie snorted, laid her small hand on his shoulder, but didn't contradict.

Winter gulped. "Stop staring at my mouth. It won't make me say anything different. I can't give you what you want. What you deserve."

"Liar, old man." She stroked the thin line between his lips with the tip of her pinkie. "You want me, and I feel the same. I'm not a child. Spill, Winter. Truth. What's the big deal?"

"Wherever this, us, might go, I am damn certain I can't do forever." Fuck, he wanted this woman more than the air mysteriously AWOL from the room.

A smile tugged at the corner of her mouth. "For heaven's sake, I'm not expecting a ring, but I sure as heck am hanging out for some good lovin', and every girly bone in my body says bad sex is not your problem. So, try again."

"I'm a relic, sweetheart, who has lived stuff you cannot imagine. You're smart, funny, and brave. The way you handled yourself in Pakistan took off-the-charts courage. Hell. You asked. The truth? I'm scared."

"I don't believe it." She grasped his hands and softly kissed the knuckles.

"Yeah. A shaking in my cowboy boots coward. Because if we start this, my gut tells me I won't want to let you go. And that terrifies this loner. My work doesn't play nice with happy families. As tempting as that thought might be, every time I look at you."

"Don't be dumb, Winter. Give us a chance. I will tie you to this bed if that's what it takes. Are you ticklish? I hope so." She leaned into him, surrounding him with her sweet, citrus smell, bathing him in the sea-blue of her eyes.

You are a goner, buddy. Crazy for her. Unable to keep his hands off her any longer, he drew her to him and kissed her as though his life depended on it.

"Make love to me," she demanded. Quietly.

A gentle push and she lay flat on her back. Circling her wrists with his fingers, he placed them above her head. "Leave your hands there." Her eyes glinted. Winter clenched his jaw, tightened the rein on his control, and took his sweet time undoing the button and lowering the zipper. Then in one move, he grabbed the sides and tugged her jeans and her panties to her ankles and onto the floor. A fucking goddess, naked below the waist, she nibbled the tip of her thumb and smiled. "Damn, Maggie King. You will be the death of my pathetic ass."

CHAPTER
TWENTY-THREE

"PATHETIC OR NOT, Winter. Don't die on me now." Maggie held her breath. Torture, keeping her hands where Winter demanded she leave them when she desperately wanted to rip his shirt off and touch his amazing body. Run her fingers over his skin, taste him. Knowing how much he wanted her, understanding his command was as much to help him take things slow made her wet.

"Hang on."

Winter cradled her against him and stood. "Where are we going?" she squealed.

"My room. The bed's bigger."

"Good thinking for an old guy," she gasped between giggles.

"Okay, smartass. You sure you're okay with this? Us?" he asked.

Sweet man. Hadn't she begged him to ravage the hell out of her? Breathing hard, she pinched his earlobe. "Idiot."

Winter lowered her feet slowly to the floor beside his

bed. The fullness of his arousal stroked across her pelvis and naval. Even through his jeans, she could tell he was bigger than her two previous lovers, plus she hadn't been with anyone since the murders.

"Top off. Let me see your breasts."

Maggie groaned. "Let, Winter? Still holding back." She did as he asked and tossed her T-shirt and bra over his head and across the room, along with her doubts about whether she could take him. "Your turn."

His lips hovered over hers. "I want to make sure we're clear, Maggie. One night. No promises."

"Yes." Butt naked, she grinned, more focused on getting Winter horizontal than what may or may not happen after. "Take off your pants." She lowered her voice and drew her eyebrows together, trying to sound as powerful as Winter.

First came his shirt. Each agonising twist of every button made her flush. Finally, when an erect honey-brown nipple appeared, she had to touch him. Lowering her hand, she stroked the long, thick erection crowding the front of his jeans.

"Christ, Maggie. Tell me you're not a virgin."

And what if she was? Did Winter have a personal code that said no virgins? "Why? she blurted, shaking her head.

"Then we definitely can't do this." Winter stroked her cheek.

"Oh, for fuck's sake." She didn't swear often, but he was tugging a very short rope. He smiled and cocked his head. "No, I'm not a virgin. I had sex my first year of college." This felt more like another job interview than their first intimate moment until she caught the tender look in his eye. Her heart swelled with physical desire and something else. A runaway flutter low in her belly that should scare her, warn her, made her want him more. "Please, don't make me wait any longer."

With a crooked smile, he kicked off his boots, lost his shirt and jeans, and twirled his jocks in the air.

"Oh, my God. Do you know how ridiculous you look?" Her breasts weren't huge, but she laughed so hard they jiggled. Embarrassed, her hands flew to cover them, finger and thumb coming together to pinch her nipples. "Ride 'em, cowboy."

"You first." He circled her wrists with his long fingers and placed her hands back above her head. "Never hide those beautiful tits from me, sweetheart."

His gaze dropped to her breasts, and what might sound crude coming from someone else turned her on more. Maggie arched, bringing her nipples closer to his mouth, and left Winter to take over. To pinch and suck. A low groan mingled with her gasps, appreciating the orgasm growing deep in her pelvis.

Eager to have him share the same rush, she dragged her hands from over her head and fumbled between them for his cock.

"Keep that up, and things will escalate." His voice rumbled in her ear.

"Going up." The rest of her sentence caught in her throat as in one very well practiced move he lifted her up and rolled underneath her. The tingling below her waist felt great, but she craved more. And judging from Winter's smoldering dark eyes, he agreed. "I want you, Winter. Now."

"You wanted to ride, sweetheart. Still feel the same way?"

Her cheeks were on fire. She wasn't a virgin, but the two lovers before Winter had preferred their women beneath them. "God, I want to, hard and fast, but I don't want to mess it up."

"You won't. Anything you need. Ask. There's nothing sexier than when you show me how to please you."

That's a first. Please her? She would have laughed if Winter's fingers hadn't found her clit. "Thanks to your very experienced fingers, Winter, I'm almost there."

His eyes glinted. Lips parted, his breath danced with the stray hair tickling the side of her mouth. He lifted it with his finger and tucked it behind her ear.

"I want this to be good for you, Maggie. Tell me what you want." Large, powerful hands stroked her sides and down her hips.

"Press. Here." She grabbed Winter's hand and pressed his rough palm to her sex. "After I come once, slide your cock inside me and fuck me until we come together." Wow! Her top fantasy spilled all over a man she hardly knew, but was damn sure had the skill to do exactly what she asked.

"Fuck me." Winter gasped.

"No. Together." Fast losing her confidence, she fell against his chest.

"No. Don't do that. Look at me."

He pressed the heel of his hand into her pelvis and curled one long finger over her clit. Maggie jerked upright, stared at the blue dots swimming on the ceiling, and lost herself in the way his finger moved in a circle faster, harder. "I think I'm co..., she rasped.

"Shh, sweetheart. Be quiet now and enjoy."

He pinched her clit and the bundle of nerves exploded, catching her somewhere between a laugh and a flood of tears. Not wanting the sensation to stop, she rode his hand.

At the peak of her release, Winter raised himself onto his elbows, took his erect shaft in his hand, and stroked from root to tip. "Let me." She scooted back so she could lick the drop of pre-cum from his cock. Salty, male. All Winter.

"Hold on, sweetheart." He steadied her waist, rolled over, opened the bedside table drawer, and took out a condom.

Eyes never leaving her face, he broke the foil with his teeth and rolled the condom over his cock. Mouth curled into that cocky grin, he flipped her onto her back, spread her legs and with a single thrust buried himself inside her.

Maggie held her breath, closed her eyes and adjusted to his size. Stretched to the max, she raised her head and collided with his mouth. A kiss that meant everything and nothing consumed them both.

"Christ, sweetheart, you're so tight," Winter growled.

"Two lovers and no sex in, er, a while, will do it to a gal." She grabbed his shoulders, pulling him towards her for another kiss. "Please don't stop."

"I can't promise I'll be gentle, but I swear I will do my best not to hurt you," Winter said.

She pressed her finger to his lips. "Enough talking. I love that you care but fuck me already."

"Goddamn it, Maggie." He bit her earlobe, slid almost all the way out, then thrust into her.

Each time fiercer than the last. Hard, like she'd asked. Firecrackers exploded in every nerve in her body. She writhed underneath him. Cried out for more and raised her head to watch his cock pumping into her. "Oh, God." She was close. "Winter?" His breath hitched and fell, soft curses tumbling over his lips.

Gymnastics had never been her strong point, but with superpower speed, she shoved him flat and straddled his hips. She ran her palms over his muscled pecs, dug her fingers into the dark smattering of coarse hair on his chest, and sank down on his erect cock.

"Fuck, yeah," he growled and grabbed her hips. "That's it, take me."

She shivered. Not sure if she could go through with this and please him as much as he did her.

"Ride me, sweetheart. Yeah, slow like that." He jerked his hips upward, finding a deep spot inside her that robbed her of breath.

They moved as one, finding a rhythm that swiftly brought them both to the edge.

"Look at me. Don't come until I say," he demanded. No sugar-coated, half-assed apology now, and she loved it.

Her body took over, clenching and squeezing him as the knot deep in her core tightened, and their coupling grew more erratic. She sucked him deeper. The walls of her vagina on fire, desperate for release. Winter's hands slowed her hips.

"Now, Maggie. Come for me."

Her breath caught in her chest, light shot through the pinholes dancing in her vision, and she dived into helpless bliss. Tears rolled down her cheeks, screaming Winter's name as he pounded through her orgasm.

"Maggie." With a loud shout, he followed.

Eventually, his thrusts slowed. Exhausted, her head slumped onto his chest. Winter pulled her close and held her tight, soothing fingers caressed up and down her spine until their breathing softened and their hearts stopped racing. *Bull crap. Once?*

CHAPTER
TWENTY-FOUR

I SWEAR that old lady with the mutt walks by one more time, I will gut her dog. Enjoy the ball of fluff's screams as I dig the knife in and paint the street with its mangy ass. It's too hard to hide my laugh, a good chuckle like I missed locked up in Souza. Thanks to Miss-Sweet-as-molasses, Sharpe. Or Maggie King, as she's calling herself these days.

I've spent over an hour sitting here watching, waiting for her to get out of bed and the curtains haven't twitched. Inside with big boy, his cock as long as my arm, fucking like rabbits.

My head is half out the window of the car ready to yell, "Party's over," when the old lady calls to the mutt. Aware my enthusiasm for this shit can escape my control, I uncurl my fingers from the door handle and shove my hand in my pocket.

Another round of paintball could be fun. Seeing the fear on the big guy's face when he thought the bitch had copped a bullet in the chest—awesome! I'll fall asleep picturing that moment for a long time.

If I had been quicker at Food Bazaar the other day, I wouldn't be sitting here, my brain turning to shit. I was close enough to shiv her right there in the cheese aisle. No one would have noticed, and she'd never have heard me coming. The damn century she took choosing fucking Pringles, I could have killed her a thousand times over.

I won't pretend it's easy, but I won't make my final move yet. No, I've got something very particular planned for that shithead Steve's sister. And there ain't nothing big boy can do to stop me. But no use letting my morning go to waste. Before I leave, I have a special present for Maggie.

Time to stretch the legs. "Buenos dias, senora." The meddler with the mutt returns my smile with a skanky nod. Not fooling her. She just hasn't made up her mind how evil I am. "Hi pooch." Avoiding its beady eyes, I pat the dog on the head.

Dumb, pint-sized alpha decides I'm no threat and nuzzles its wet nose against my leg. Talk about skin crawl, and the old lady isn't quick enough to stop me from pulling one of its ears, which earns me a nip. Worth it to see its eyes roll.

"*Buenos Dias*. You looking for someone?" She gathers the mutt in her arms and raises a possessive nose at the brownstone next door to the bitch and her mate. "I live here. Can I help you?"

"Damn glasses! *Perdóname, senora*." Ugh. I want to stick my fingers down my throat, but my mom taught me you catch more flies with sugar than vinegar. "Must have left them at home. There should be a spare pair in the car, but I can't seem to find them." I peer at the brownstone door. "This is a two-eleven, right?"

"No," she says, scanning me up and down.

Scrambling to get back on the ground and onto its skinny legs, her dog has shifted to yipping attack mode. Fucking hilarious.

"Two-eleven is further along."

"Okay, thanks. *Gracias*." The fat heifer isn't warming to me, so I reckon it's best I take off for now. "You have a good day." Nosy bitch, I wouldn't put it past her to call the cops.

As I drive away, she's talking to the mutt. The triumphant smirk on her dumb face says, strike one for neighborhood watch. I'll let it go, because when I rock up to the finish line, it will be epic.

A quick swing around the block because there's one more goodie to drop before we end this. *Bueno*. No sign of Senora Busybody. Finally, the gods are smiling my way. The small package should fit easily in the mailbox. Shit, I'm grinning again. This is turning out to be one hell of a fucking good day.

CHAPTER
TWENTY-FIVE

MAGGIE DUCKED under Winter's arm and stepped into the Sentinel offices, grumble bear hot on her heels, the small of his hand guiding her towards reception. First day back at the office and although they hadn't really talked about it, she knew he was nervous, and at the same time glad to return to the action.

While she waited for Winter, she'd checked the mailbox. The rain had stopped, but the weatherman promised more later and the last thing she wanted to find when they got home was a soggy delivery of yarn. As soon as she laid eyes on the envelope, the hairs on the back of her neck spiked. Lazenby. Memories of the old days, his threats, turned her blood cold.

While they drove to work, it made sense to tell Winter, but she hadn't liked to spoil his grumble. Like Sam, he enjoyed ranting at the bridge traffic. Over mid-morning coffee would be soon enough, she decided.

"Well, howdy stranger." Linda came from behind her desk and linked arms with Winter.

She sounded like something out of a fifties cowboy movie. "Morning, Linda," Maggie said with an equally faked smile on her face.

Winter flicked a glance between them and frowned. For such a good looking man, she found it hard to believe he didn't get Linda's game. Or maybe there was nothing to get, and she was overreacting.

"How's the arm?"

Apparently, the question required lots of arm stroking. Maggie swallowed, determined not to give into the green-eyed monster and bite, and inwardly smiled when Winter untethered his arm and grabbed her hand.

"Just fine, Linda. Any messages?" he grumbled.

"A few. But I'll deal with them. My pleasure to take care of you."

Ugh. Do you have no pride? If Linda wasn't so goddam irritating, Maggie should feel sorry for her instead of wishing she'd fall through a hole in the floor.

"Snake wants to see you. He's in the briefing room."

"Yeah. Okay." Winter called over his shoulder, one hand on her back as he let Maggie along the hallway.

"No. Not you." Linda screeched. "Sorry. Just Winter."

Heart sinking, Maggie sighed. Showing him Lazenby's note could wait until he finished. Not like they were going anywhere.

"Shouldn't be long, sweetheart." He cupped the back of her neck and kissed her forehead.

"No problem. But if I'm not needed, I think I'll go on uptown and do some shopping. I can take the bus home."

Winter shook his head. *No fucking way* etched into his brow.

Maggie grinned. Message received. "Okay. Good thing I have my knitting." She waved her bag. "I'll check into the kitchen and wait for you there."

"Soon, sweetheart." He kissed her again and was gone.

Late morning, Sentinel should be buzzing. When they weren't out in the field, the team spent their time interviewing new clients, and sorting the priority list while Snake had top-level meetings with men and women dressed in black suits who entered through the back door.

Almost as big as her studio apartment in Boston, Sentinel's kitchen had all the latest gizmos, waffle makers, juicers, and a coffee machine a person needed a pilot's licence to operate.

Maggie's hand trembled as she poured her third cup of the day. Already a bag of nerves, the extra caffeine wouldn't help. She glanced over her shoulder, half-expecting to see Winter. The first time he saw her dunk a chocolate chip cookie into her coffee, he'd been horrified, but the soggy sugar comfort hit was exactly what she needed.

She did a quick wipe around the shelves, thankful she had something to keep her busy, before she grabbed her coffee in one hand, chocolate chip cookie in the other, slumped into a chair and placed them on the break table.

Holding her breath, she gingerly plucked Lazenby's envelope out of her pocket and stared at his note. Reading the words a hundred times didn't change a thing. They stayed the same. Her teeth gnawed at her bottom lip, the salty taste of blood rolling over her tongue, and she struggled to crank down the tears. Folded neatly inside the note were Steve's dog tags.

Her brother never took them off, but they had disappeared the night of the shooting. *Thought you might want to give these to Steve. Won't be long before you all catch up. Make sure you say hi to that hoe, Jody for me. Can't wait to see her again.*

How had Lazenby found her? For the life of her she didn't know, only knew for sure that he had. Kenny and her old professor were the only two people who knew her real last name.

Tears had to go somewhere, and unfortunately, Maggie's streamed from her nose. With a sniff, she cuffed them and shoved the note and tags back into her pocket.

She got why Snake didn't want her to the meeting, Sentinel always had another job running or in the planning stage, and after Pakistan, she'd experienced enough of death and violence for three lifetimes. Not wanting to make it all about her, she picked up her knitting and hoped the meeting didn't go too long.

A smile crept over her cheeks. Last night, Winter had found pleasure spots on her body she never guessed she had. But the things she loved most about him went way beyond passionate sex. At least for her. Him, not so much, she suspected. Which didn't do much for her confidence, no matter how much she told herself she knew the score and had agreed not to care. Not too much, anyway.

Maggie rolled her eyes. One day, she would figure out how to stop her yarn and brain from getting tangled in knots. A major overspend at Knit and Stitch, but the feel and color of the yarns were irresistible. Cable patterns were never her strong point, but she was determined to master it. The twirly design was the perfect way to show off the aqua and purple chosen for Sam's sweater.

Most days, the click-clack of the needles calmed her, but today they wove a tangled ball of yuck memories in her head. She had half a mind to call Detective Esposito, but Winter might not appreciate cops banging on his door without a clue what was going on.

Occasionally, she wished her growly bear missed a beat, added salt instead of sugar to his coffee. Even if she adored the way he watched out for her. Checking to see if she'd eaten. Was she too hot, too cold? Leaving a light on when it got dark.

Some people might find it over the top, claustrophobic, but after five years of living alone, no one to share stuff with, allowing him to take charge of some minor details of her life, relaxed her. If she asked, he gave her space.

This last week he hadn't complained once about his shoulder, but the tight lines around his mouth and the way he rubbed his forehead when he thought she wasn't looking said he still had pain. Tonight, maybe she'd try taking control. Order him to lie back and enjoy.

Not much in the mood for knitting today, Maggie gave up and shoved it into her bag. Instead of sitting there stressing about Lazenby, she should do something useful. Clear her head. Linda usually collected everyone's lunch from the deli at the end of the street. She could give her a break and offer to collect the takeout. That might make up for being jealous over nothing earlier.

Out front, Linda sat at her desk, painting her nails. So much for being up to her neck in paperwork. "Wow. They look amazing. No chance of me growing mine that long. They split and crack. What's your secret?" Maggie leaned over the counter.

Linda raised her head. "Show me."

Straight to the chase. The guys liked her directness. It meant they didn't have to waste time spelling stuff out, and Maggie wished she thought the same, but the woman's tone grated. She crumbled inside whenever Linda spoke to her, convinced she had done something wrong, but she'd asked, so she popped her hands in front of her.

"You bite them?" Linda asked.

"Er, yes, sometimes," Maggie curled her fingers. "I'd love to hear your tips on stopping, but not today. I came to ask if you'd do me a favour and let me collect the lunch order. Stop me from being bored out of my mind."

"Well. I have a bunch of emails to send this afternoon, and Winter asked me to type a report for him." Linda straightened her spine, tightened the top of the nail polish bottle, and tossed it into her drawer. "For my eyes only."

Since when? "So let me help. Waiting for him is driving me crazy." Quickly, Maggie ducked her head, afraid Linda might hear her teeth grinding together.

"Okay, fine. The deli rang. It's ready. Tell them you're from Sentinel. No need to pay. Snake takes care of the tab at the end of the month."

Finally, Linda smiled. She had a brilliant smile. Should do it more often. "Great. I won't be long," Maggie sang out and headed out the door.

Fresh air was good for you, she repeated to herself while ignoring the chilly wind nipping her nose and numbing her toes. She patted her jacket, looking for her cell to send Winter a text, let him know where she had gone. Too bad she had left it in her knitting bag. Middle of the day. Plenty of people. If she took the shortcut through the small park, she could make it back before the meeting ended. A couple of guys by the small fountain were playing drums for a tap dancer. Maggie chuckled. A dollar said his feet were warm.

She'd slowed to watch when her stomach started to ache. The nagging torture that had been the norm during the days of Lazenby's trial. Pivoting slowly, she checked out the park. No sight of him didn't mean he wasn't lurking somewhere. Maggie picked up her pace, dread snaking through her gut until she broke into a jog.

The kids tossing a ball whizzed past in a blur. Certain the iron gate in the distance was the exit opposite the deli, she angled toward it. Out of nowhere, a mountain of green flew at her. Arms flying, her head hit the ground before her butt, and her eyes watered. Face hidden under his hoodie, her assailant cursed. Not too tall. Not Lazenby unless he'd lost a lot of weight.

Her nerves frazzled beyond repair, Maggie opened her mouth to bawl him out. Except it was her fault. Not watching where she was going and fantasizing about boogie men. In any case, the skateboarder didn't hang around to apologize.

A few people stared, but no one offered to help. Oddly, she was grateful for no fuss, but not ready to try standing just yet. She took a long, steadying breath and took a few seconds for her stomach to settle. Blood trickled down her calf from a nasty cut on her knee. Unlikely there were any broken bones. Still, she wiggled her toes and circled her ankles.

A couple of deeper breaths and she could stand. Blurred vision and her thumping head made walking in a straight line difficult. Must have banged her head harder than she thought. Dumb not going back for her phone. Hands wrapped around her torso, Maggie willed the creepy sensation circling her tail bone to take a hike and focused on making it across to the deli. Her feet made it through the door, but she wasn't confident they'd take her much further when the guy behind the counter came to check on her.

"Here, lady, sit down. You look like you're going to pass out. Joe. Get her a glass of water," he yelled at the older man fixing sandwiches.

Before she did faint, she grabbed his forearm and gasped, "Can I borrow your cell?"

"Sure thing." He reached under his apron and handed it to her.

"Thanks." What a mess. Linda was the last person she wanted to call, but her head wouldn't stop spinning. Willing her hand to stop shaking while she dialed, she sucked in a breath and held on tight.

"Good afternoon, Sentinel Security," Linda chirped.

"Hi. It's me, Maggie. Sorry to bug you. Er, I have had an accident. Nothing serious, but I'm a little lightheaded and worried that I'll drop everyone's lunch if I try to carry back to the office." Maggie winced at the pain behind her eyeballs. Mainly from embarrassment at being such a klutz. "I'm fine, and I don't like to ask you, but I left my phone behind. Can you call an Uber to come get me and the food?" she pleaded, but the line went dead.

CHAPTER
TWENTY-SIX

WINTER SHOOK his head as he wandered out of Snake's office. Gee, it was great to be back in the center of the action, feel the blood pumping, anticipation of the upcoming mission. As soon as Snake's meeting began, he had his game face on, and that was the way it should be. His brothers depended on him to get shit right the first time.

Storm had updated him on Maggie's background check. It had only been a couple of weeks, even though it felt like a lifetime ago when he had asked him. His teammate reported *nada*—nothing on her beyond the past five years. No parking tickets, credit card debt. Zip. He wanted to give her a chance to explain. That's why he'd asked Storm to hold off and not probe any deeper.

He headed to the kitchen. An apology on his lips for keeping her waiting. A drag hanging around but going back to Brooklyn on her own was never an option.

Winter never imagined he'd fall hard for any woman. Ever since Smiley died, he committed to the bachelor life-style. Then along came Maggie, and he couldn't string a sensible sentence together whenever they were within two feet of each other. But the unsaid, big stuff, kept on building.

Take this morning. Something changed between letting her escape from the shower, not easy when he wanted to carry her wet, warm body back to his bed and keep her there for at least the next three weeks, and when he caught up with her sitting in his vehicle, locked up tighter than Fort Knox. Not a single word as they drove into Manhattan.

Sex with Maggie was off the fucking charts amazing, the best, and these past few days a tenderness he reckoned long gone from his repertoire, had crept into bed with them. Despite what he'd said, long term with this beautiful woman might work.

Nights with Maggie, under him, on top of him, any place she'd have him, and stuff had shifted. Deep in his core, he imagined they had a chance.

If doubting his commitment was why she looked so fucking miserable, he needed to clear that shit up pronto and hope she saw him in her future. They could work it out, handle the serious decisions. Maggie would be alongside him on many Sentinel missions, but could she cope with the times when he flew solo, incommunicado, with no return date marked on the calendar? Tonight, while he sucked on her delicious earlobe, they'd talk.

Yeah. Winter's smile left his face as soon as he poked his head into the kitchen. *Where the hell is she?* The hairs on his forearm spiked. Not a good sign.

"Hey, Linda. You seen Maggie?" he hollered at the front desk.

"Yes. She left half an hour ago to pick up everyone's lunch. I expected her back by now."

He held back the curse on the tip of his tongue. Collecting their food order was Linda's job, not Maggie's. "Why did she go?"

"She insisted. I tried to stop her, but she insisted, and I don't like to argue." Linda cocked her head and batted her false eyelashes at him.

Maggie should have let him know she'd left Sentinel. They'd agreed while dicks with paintball guns roamed the streets and forklift trucks mysteriously showed up out of nowhere. They'd agreed. She should have sent him a text.

Winter chuckled. No getting round the age gap. He sounded more like her father than her lover. Vaguely aware of the reception phone ringing, he took out his cell and checked his messages. He'd give Maggie hell when he saw her. Yeah, for the length of a heartbeat. First, she needed to waltz through the door.

"Yes, yes. Of course? Someone will be right there," Linda said, frantically waving at him.

His chest tightened. Two strides and he stood smack in the middle of Linda's space. "Tell me." Her eyes widened. *Shit.* He stepped back. "What's happened?"

"There's been an accident. At the deli."

Winter grabbed the counter to stop himself from shaking, fearing the worst, as Sam barrelled toward them.

"It's Maggie."

"Winter? Sam laid her finger on his arm.

"Not now." He shrugged her off, getting to Maggie the only thing he had headspace for right now.

"It's not my fault," Linda wailed.

Like hell it's not. Unreasonable? Sure. But he wasn't sticking around to apologize. Without wasting another

158

second, he made straight for the door. Getting his vehicle would waste time, so he started running. Feet pounding the sidewalk, stroke for stroke matched his thumping heart.

Winter stilled his hand on the deli door and peered through the glass. He couldn't see Maggie, only Frank bending over someone at a corner table, but it had to be her. Bursting in Terminator style might scare her, so he steeled his anxious gut and exhaled. Frank turned, immediately recognised him, moved aside, and made way for Winter to crouch in front of her.

"Hi," she said, lifting her head.

Warning bells clanged, but he breathed a little easier knowing she was conscious, even if he didn't like the faraway look in her eyes. "Hi, sweetheart. What happened?"

"Had an argument with a skateboard. My fault, I wasn't looking where I was going," she sniffed.

It took everything in him to shut down the sarcasm roaring in his throat. *What is it with you and wheels? Skateboards, fucking forklifts?* Worried if he took her in his arms, he'd never to let her out of his sight ever again, he forced his hands to his side. "How are you feeling? Think you can walk?"

"Shaky, but okay." She shivered. "My head hurts."

Winter slipped off his coat and dropped it over her shoulders. Ignoring her protest, and the fact the whole knight in fucking shining armor thing was getting to be a habit, he helped her out of the chair. "Appreciate you taking care of her, Frank. Do me a favor and call Linda. Have her collect the food. The guys are starving."

"No problem, Winter. You look after the little lady. I'll send someone. Take care, Miss."

"'Preciate it." Winter nodded, squeezed Maggie's hand, and forced a grin.

"Where are we going?" she asked.

"To the hospital to get you checked out." Colliding with a skateboarder probably had inflicted no serious injuries, but he had to be sure.

"No. I'm okay. A bit bruised, but fine. Please, Winter, can we go home?"

One look at her trembling bottom lip and the tear rolling across her pale cheek, and making her smile soared to priority status. He'd take the risk. "Sure, sweetheart. Hang on tight to my arm." Home. Hell, that shouldn't have such a sweet ring to it.

CHAPTER
TWENTY-SEVEN

RIDING the rollercoaster of her queasy stomach, Maggie gripped the strap swinging above her and focused on the road. It didn't help. The traffic swapping lanes at speed made her head spin. Winter's large hand covered hers. She gave her fingers a wiggle and appreciated his comforting squeeze.

"Not long, sweetheart. Hang in there, and we'll soon have you resting in bed."

"Uh-huh." She didn't dare nod in case she vomited. Winter had a frown on his face and wished she wasn't always, at least that's how it felt, the cause.

A few doors down from his house, he rolled the truck to a gentle halt. Lucky. Often, they walked a block from where they parked. *Home.* The word had been swimming around in the mush inside her head. Truth, the longer she spent at Winter's, the less she wanted to leave.

Whatever was going on between them started with the promise of one night. An agreement to see where time took them. Despite being pretty sure forever sounded good to her, she couldn't be certain Winter was reading the same page.

"Wait there. I'm coming to you," he said.

His grip tightened on her fingers, his gaze lingering a breath before he opened his door and came around to her side. The sweet man hadn't let her feet touch the ground since they left the deli. Why not enjoy the ride? Her head flopped against his chest.

The mattress dipped as he carefully laid her on it, the squeaking bedframe reminding her of the steady rhythm of their lovemaking last night. She shivered.

"You, cold, baby?" Winter stroked the hair from her eyes. "I can fix that."

Of course he could. Turning on the gas fire, and much more. A soft, orange glow pulsed off the walls and ceiling, instantly taking the chill from her body. It had stopped raining, but the wind still had a bite to it.

"Mmm. That's great. You sincerely are a treasure. Thank you for coming to get me." Along with her pounding head, her eyelids drooped. "I need to tell you something. This morning, I…"

"Shh." He brushed his thumb over the inside of her wrist. "Rest, you're not going anywhere, while I go find the first-aid kit and clean that cut on your forehead. I'll check your knee, too."

That crease was back between his eyebrows. "Don't over-think it, Winter. My head will not fall off from a nasty bruise."

"It's up to you. Either I look at it, or I change my mind and we take that trip to the E. R."

"Okay. I give up. Any chance of a glass of water while

you're out there fishing for bandages?" She couldn't resist giving him a nudge with her toe. He snagged her foot and slipped off her shoes. "Oh, you are so sweet."

"You slay me, Maggie. Sweet? Treasure? Wrong guy. But now it's my turn to take care of you."

As if he had ever stopped. "You are a drama queen. They shot you. I had a run-in with a skateboarder. Can't compare the two."

The pads of his fingers massaged the sole of her foot. Blissed out by the way his fingers massaged the sole of her foot, dug deeper into her arches. Firm, but gentle. "Oh, my God, I am melting."

"Good. Rest. I'll get the kit and water."

One eye open, she watched him leave. Graceful strides ate the space he owned in every way. Overwhelmed by the past few hours, she closed her eyes and followed her breath. A trick the audiologist suggested to help with the fear of not being able to hear well.

She had an app on her phone that worked, too. Thank heaven, Winter had brought her cell. He'd said nothing about her forgetting to take it with her. Yet. Breathing deeply, she swallowed her nausea, hitched her elbow under her side for support, grasped the knitting bag Winter had placed at the end of the bed, and took out Lazenby's note.

Suddenly, she couldn't wait to tell him and needed to be close to Winter. Head swimming, she got up and went to find him. Her balance off, as she stumbled into the kitchen.

"Steady." Winter caught her elbow a second before she fell and pulled her to his side. "What are you doing here? Remember what you told me? Rest is the same in any language."

Before he could scoop her into his arms, she lurched out of his grasp. "I'm going to be sick," she croaked, waving her hand at him, forbidding him to follow to the bathroom. She made it to the toilet a second before he kneeled next to her and drew slow circles on her upper back.

"Go away," Maggie whined. Far from being comforting, having Winter this close while she puked was mortifying.

"Easy. I'm not going anywhere." Winter brushed the hair from her face and handed her a washcloth.

Brimming with concern, his eyes had turned the color of dark molasses, and like he promised, he stayed until she stopped heaving. It would take more energy than she had to crawl to the bedroom, so she eased her backside onto the tiled floor, secretly glad when Winter sat next to her. He cupped her cheek with his palm and tucked her head into the soft space beneath his armpit. "Sorry."

"Shh. You're not the first person I've seen puke."

"You often say the sweetest things, but that was not one of them." Maggie sniffed.

"Hold still. I want to look at that cut."

Maggie didn't have the energy to object. Tiny balls of bright light circled behind her eyelids as he ran the pad of his thumb across her eyebrow, grazing the edges of the gash. "How's it look?" She winced.

Air whistled between his teeth. "Not bad, but…"

"You are lousy at this. Tell me." One eye crinkled shut, the other cracked open, she raised her gaze to the ceiling as if she had a hope in hell of checking for herself. "Damn. It needs stitches."

"Fraid so, sweetheart. E.R.?"

Maggie shook her head, giving the eyeball elf its cue to

hammer. She grabbed Winter's hand. "No, please." Her last trip to a hospital, the half-way house to hell, Steve was hooked up to noisy machines. When the doctor pulled the plug, she vowed on the final beep, never to set foot in one ever again. Aside from her hearing check-ups at a clinic, she'd succeeded. "Please. I can't go there." She dug her nails into his palm.

"Okay. Take it easy. I'll call Jenna."

"No. Bothering her is just as bad. It's late. Her kid will be home from school, wanting food."

"Not a problem. Today's Thursday. Storm takes him to the gym after school."

"My lucky day." She hadn't realised Storm and Jenna were close. Mainly because as a newcomer, too, Maggie assumed Jenna didn't know the guys real well.

"Come on. Let's get you back to bed, and I'll call."

He placed one arm under her knees and the other around her waist and lifted her into his arms. Too damn exhausted to keep protesting, with a deep sigh, she sank into Winter's strength. Enjoy, she ordered herself, because soon she'd have a place of her own, and not seeing him would claim a huge chunk from her happiness budget.

CHAPTER
TWENTY-EIGHT

WINTER LED Jenna to the door, grateful she'd taken the time to check on Maggie, but not surprised. The team looked out for each other. He'd do the same for her anytime. Hell, he and his Sentinel brothers would lay down their lives for the other. A fact proven repeatedly on various missions. Not that anyone had ever died, but they'd all stepped up to the test.

"Thanks, Jenna, 'preciate you stopping by."

"No problem." She grabbed his hand and pulled him in for a hug before he took his next breath.

Storm was a lucky man, and he nearly told Jenna just that until he remembered, technically, they hadn't mentioned being in any kind of relationship. He grinned, his chin digging deeper into her shoulder. They way the two looked at each other, it weren't no secret.

"Take care of our girl, Winter." Jenna dropped her hands from his neck and took off down the stairs.

"I will. Drive safely, you hear?"

"Always. Go on inside before you catch pneumonia."

No way. With all the crazy stuff going on around Maggie right now, he kept his eyes on the doc until she was in her car and driving toward the bridge. Before he closed the door, he did a quick recon, made sure no Buicks lurked, that the shadows under the streetlight illuminated nothing but dancing leaves.

He was still kicking himself for not taking Maggie straight to the hospital. Either the woman was uber accident prone or she had an aggressive stalker. He'd bet the rest of his grandfather's fortune the past three physical hits weren't personal. She denied it, but Kenny loomed large in the frame. Tonight, she was safe in bed, resting. Super glued to her side, any unlikely intruder would have to go through him to get to her. Telling her now might make her more anxious. But tomorrow, like he should have done after the fucking paintball malarky, he'd pay Kenny a visit and sort his skinny ass.

Concussions were nasty. Any wonder Maggie had a splitting headache. Winter climbed onto the bed and lay beside her. He reached for her hand and turned to look at her. Paler than before, her eyelids fluttered, and he got mad all over again. His temple pounding. If it wasn't Kenny, then good thing the person who'd knocked her down hadn't stopped and left his number.

"Hey, sweetheart. Talk to me." He shook her arm. Jenna had emphasised how important it was that Maggie didn't nod off for long stretches.

"Ow! Please, Winter. I just want to sleep."

"I know. Jenna's coming back tomorrow. If she gives you the okay, I promise, you can doze for a week. One more time. What happened today?"

167

"Jeez. You're pushy," she slurred.

"My middle name. This skateboarder. Was it a man, a woman, tall, short, fat, thin? Hair color?" He hated badgering, watching her teeth scrape her lower lip as she fought back the fog and tried to remember.

"Male, not very big. Don't see guys your size zipping through parks on one of those things. He didn't hang around to debate who was at fault. Sorry." Maggie rubbed her scrunched face.

"Why are you sorry? Irresponsible jerk. Hey, look at me. Wanna hear a story?" His gaze shot to the bookcase. She'd read to him plenty when he acted like a baby over his sore arm. Time to return the favor. There had to be something on his shelf she'd like.

"No thanks. Sorry."

"Stop with the apologies, sweetheart. If me reading doesn't appeal, name your tune," he pushed, waving his hand at the row of album covers. Not that she was looking. He shook her gently until her pretty blue eyes opened.

"Music. Now, you are spoiling me."

Maggie half smiled, and Winter's breath lodged against what felt like a fishbone stuck in the center of his chest.

"Got any Nina Simone?"

"I like it. Into the classics." Winter arrowed straight for his favorite, *Wild is the Wind*, relieved she hadn't requested Black Pink. When he took Linda to dinner, she talked about the girl band all night, considered it important he was on board with their hot comeback.

Nothing wrong with her enthusiasm. He still had a lot to learn about and Maggie, but he already knew she and Linda rocked to a different tune on many levels. Then it hit him, drowned by a fucking emotional tsunami. This woman, the one lying by his side, nursing the headache from hell, worrying the shit out of him, lightened his soul.

Her touch, lips, eyes. The sway of her sexier than hell hips? Much younger, with an unjaded lens on life. He didn't have a clue how, only that she had captured whatever masqueraded as his heart, teasing him with possibility every time a second ticked. This woman who healed wounds with Disney Band-Aids and woolly hats.

Every hour he spent with her, his desire to have her deep inside his skin grew stronger. With the edge of his thumb, Winter flicked the hair from her eyes and brought his mouth to her ear. "Wild is the wind," he whispered, echoing Nina Simone's riff.

CHAPTER
TWENTY-NINE

WINTER HEARD MAGGIE STIR, but he kept whisking the eggs, willing her to do to stay the hell in bed. Adding the salt and pepper, he remembered not so long ago pushing his doctor's orders, but no one said he was smarter than the woman warming his sheets?

They were both stubborn, and most of the time, Winter admired her independence. There was lots to love about Maggie King, like her special moan right before she came, the breathy groan after she did. No matter how often common sense warned him she'd be better off with someone else, his dumb heart told him to shut the fuck up and refused to listen.

Caught in Maggie's spell, getting to know everything about her quickly became his main reason for waking up in the morning, preferably with his head between her legs, tongue exploring her clit, learning, lusting, longing to keep her by his side.

Too soon? A fucking understatement. But the inevitability of being alone again in his empty house, nothing but Smiley's ghost for company, wrecked him. And as luck would have it, in the meeting yesterday, Snake had provided breathing space. He hadn't told Maggie yet, but he planned on fixing that today. She didn't have to rush to find an apartment.

Sentinel's upcoming mission meant he would be away for a while. Sad, but glad Maggie's skill set wasn't required. He didn't think he'd survive putting her in danger so soon after the last time.

She would have his home to herself, and due to the uncertainty around recent incidents, Snake had agreed to schedule someone on watch twenty-four-seven.

"Damn!" Fat from the fry pan spat in his face. Bacon and eggs always perked him up when he didn't feel too great, but with her queasy stomach, Maggie might prefer an omelette. He gripped the spatula, ready to start one when she wobbled into the kitchen.

Dark smudges under her eyes emphasised the tired creases at the corner of her mouth. He might respect her independence, the fact she didn't look for anyone to fix stuff, but one more sway and he'd haul Ms. King's fine ass back to bed.

Not a breath too soon, her shaky hand clamped the edge of the counter. Maintaining his cool, he took the pan off the heat, stepped sideways and circled her in his arms. "Morning. Feeling better?" His front pressed to her back, Winter nuzzled her ear and waited for her to lie.

She should feel like hell. Neither of them slept more than a few hours. Last night, her nightmares had kept them both awake, and when she finally drifted off, that concussion meant he woke her regularly.

"Terrible." Maggie huffed.

Honesty. Surprised, a chuckle rolled around his chest. Dazzlingly unpredictable. Had the soft, warm body tucked against him ever been anything else? Standing this close, her head grazed his chin and his cock came alive. "Sorry. I wasn't expecting you to tell me the truth."

"And that makes you hard?" She tried to wriggle away, but he placed his hands on the counter, either side of her hips, and kept her right where she was.

"No, of course not. That didn't come out right," he said, stifling that chuckle.

"Guess I am oversensitive, but what about you? How are you doing after I kept you awake all night? It's late. We should have been at work an hour ago."

Cute. Watching her nose crinkle to give her yawn space, he wondered when it would be a good time to tell her he planned on waking up beside her sleepy head every morning.

"Nope. Snake ordered us to stay away from Sentinel for the day." Reluctantly, he released his hands and poured her a coffee. They had run out of the choc chip cookies she liked. He'd fix that later. "Hungry?"

She took the mug, closed her eyes, and sniffed. "No appetite, but mmm, this coffee is perfect."

Maggie's soft lips pecked his forehead and his cock swelled with fucking pride for making a good cup of coffee. "You're perfect," he insisted. The sexiest woman he'd ever been with, and her unbrushed hedgehog hair didn't change a damn thing.

"Sit. Jenna said to take Tylenol for your headache. With food. Think you can manage some toast?"

"One slice. Don't go crazy."

Before he could insist two would be better, her cell beeped. "Phone." He pointed to the knitting bag. Not wanting anything to disturb her last night, he'd brought it upstairs with him.

"I hear it." Maggie crossed her eyes, slid her hand across the kitchen bench, and grabbed it from the bag.

Pulling on his earlobe was coming on a little strong, but she'd taken out her aid after Jenna examined her, but when she woke up, she must have seen it. An apology hovered on his lips until the teasing light playing with her mouth vanished. "Who is it?" he asked, trying to sound casual.

"Wrong number." She avoided his hand when he reached for her phone.

Fucking Kenny. "Maggie?"

"I need a shower." She shoved her half drank mug of coffee away from her and slipped off the stool.

And he let her go. Don't think for one goddam minute the conversation had finished, but he would never force her to stay. "Maggie," he repeated loudly, making sure she heard the edge in his voice.

"Not now, Winter. Let me shower, then I promise I'll share."

Winter thumped the bench and swore, separated four egg whites for her omelette and counted the seconds until she returned. By the time she wandered back into the kitchen, squeaky clean and smelling of citrus and that purple body wash stuff she used, he was slathering another slice of toast with chunky marmalade.

Maggie pulled up a stool and sat opposite him, her bottom lip trembling. Not wanting to send her running for the bathroom again, he leaned in slowly, reached for a strand of her long wet hair and dragged it behind her ear. The hearing aid was in place. "More coffee?"

"Water, thanks."

A hot shower usually relaxed them both, but the tension in the air got thicker as he filled her glass and placed two Tylenol and a slice of toast in front of her.

Her gaze met his for a second, then spiralled to the floor.

Winter cleared his throat. "We good?" he asked, fingers crossed Maggie would spill the details of the phone call.

Maggie flashed a lopsided smile that didn't reach her eyes. "Sorry I took so long. Couldn't find my damn hearing aid."

"Uh-huh." He held her gaze until she blinked. In the back of his mind, he counted the ways he'd make Kenny pay.

Bad timing, but his overactive libido craved another feel of her wild, sweet-smelling hair. To pull her close. Suck on her plump bottom lip until she begged for a kiss. Instead, he sniffed a long breath through his nose and drank in the woman staring into her water as though it contained the secrets of the universe.

With all the shit going on these past few weeks, he should give her a break, but he was done with the cat and mouse games. Done with her protecting Kenny. What did this fucking cretin mean to her?

"No more running, Maggie. As sweet as your fine ass is wiggling away, you need to trust me. Can you do that? Who called? Kenny? What does he want?" His voice got louder with every question. *Nice job reigning in control.*

But the way her body trembled was more than a reaction

to his harsh tone. "Dammit. What's wrong?" Afraid if he made any sudden move she'd run, he inched his palm along the table, across the chasm between them.

Maggie stared over his shoulder and out the window. "He's here."

That was a start. Desperate for her to share more, he interlaced their fingers and gently squeezed.

"Out there. He's watching. Said he won't wait any longer."

Her skin was ice cold. Kenny was hanging from the end of Winter's rapidly shortening fuse. God help the fucker. He raised their joined fingers to his lips and blew warm air across her knuckles. "Don't worry. I'll take care of him. Kenny won't bother you again."

"No." She wrenched from his grasp, flew out of her seat, escaped to the window and stared onto the street.

His heart hammered. If it didn't slow, he'd have a heart attack. Without waiting to be invited, he stood next to her and rested his palm lightly on her shoulder. Tears streaming over her cheeks, in between her sobs, she started signing.

"Sweetheart. I'm sorry. I don't understand." He grabbed her flying fingers and cradled them against his chest. Her head slumped against him as he sprinkled kisses across the pulse at her wrist.

"It's not Kenny," she sighed.

Christ, was she afraid of what he might do to the prick? On the edge, patience thin, he couldn't promise her fears weren't real. "You understand this is crazy. Beats me why you insist on protecting this loser, but I'm going out there to take care of this."

Maggie gripped his forearm. "You're safe here. No one

can get past the code." Slowly, but firmly, he uncurled the fingers now clutching his shirt and left.

Winter stood at the top of the stone steps, listening for any sign of the person watching the house. Nothing, only the wind rustling in the trees. A block over, someone shouted. The engine of a plane flying out of Newark airport roared overhead. Familiar sounds. No unexpected movement, except for a squirrel darting across the road. If Kenny, anyone, had been out there, they were long gone.

Winter clutched his cell, poised to bring in his team to help, when Maggie called out to him. He quickly re-set the door code and raced upstairs. She stood at the top, hands clutching the banister, trembling. "I'm here." Winter pulled her into his arms and kissed the top of her head. "There's no one out there."

For two people who had shared a lot over the last few days, they were holding back. They both sensed it was true. Scared, for different reasons or maybe the same? Who the hell knew, but her safety, any future they might have together, depended on Maggie trusting him to do what he did best. Protect her. He tucked her into his side, walked them to his couch, and sat with her on his knee. "Now, sweetheart. Talk to me. There's stuff I need to tell you, too."

CHAPTER
THIRTY

MAGGIE UNDERSTOOD men like Winter found it impossible to ignore people in trouble. It simply did not compute with their DNA—not if they had the power to help.

They were way past being strangers, and right now, unless she caught the Amtrak out of New York, and kept running, she was clueless when it came to handling Lazenby. If the cops had found him, Esposito would have called. Plus, Winter had laid everything on Kenny. Her fault, and she had no time for the weasel, but she couldn't let Winter hurt him.

"Look at me." Winter angled her chin to face him.

Mesmerized by his whiskey-colored eyes, it was impossible not to.

"I get that you're scared, but meet me halfway. Having no clue what I'm dealing with here makes it difficult to keep you safe. Worrying about you every minute of the day is killing me.

Maggie's breath hitched. The edgy frustration in Winter's voice sucked.

"Help me out. Are you sure the guy on the skateboard wasn't Kenny? If you're worried I'll kill him, that's fair. I can't deny that I'd sure as hell love to end anyone who'd hurt you."

Watching Winter's giant palm stroke up and down her body, she wished, not for the first time in her life, she was as tall as him, six feet plus and packed with toned, powerful muscle. But being the next best thing to the Hulk hadn't helped her brother. A bullet levelled big men as easily as it tore through Josie.

Maggie shuddered, imagining Winter bleeding out in a dark alley made her scared to take her next breath, move into the future.

"Keeping secrets will get you killed, Maggie, and I can't sit here waiting for that to happen."

When you couldn't hear well, you listened, more intensely than most, filtering every word someone spoke through a kind of superhero tuner. She didn't have to try too hard to catch the hint of apology lacing the urgency in his tone.

If she stayed silent, perhaps he'd let her walk away or take off and find Kenny. Worse, Lazenby killed him. Desperate to trust the grumpiest, bossiest person on the planet who was kinder to her than anyone had been since she lost Steve, Maggie swan-dived into the sanctuary of his bottomless brown eyes.

Tears latched onto the back of her throat and played tug of war. If someone ever asked her if a human heart could haemorrhage? Yes, would be her answer. God, she missed her brother.

Winter held her hips and lifted her to sit next to him. "Maggie?" Their foreheads touched.

For the past five years, Steve's murder had ruled her life. Lazenby's spit flying across the courtroom as he swore she was a dead woman remained etched on her eyeballs. Locked up in jail, with a life sentence. But she'd never been able to let go of the fear he would make good on his threats.

Running held no guarantees, and she loved making friends with Sam and Jenna. Who knew what the strong, smart women saw in her, but they liked her, and she wanted to know them better?

"Sweetheart. Listen to me." Winter tugged his earlobe, which always made her laugh. "Dammit, are you turned on?"

"Yes. I can *hear* you," she signed. Her flickering hands gave her precious seconds to figure out what to say next.

"Funny. Words. I need your words." He grabbed her fingers, a flash of anger sweeping over his craggy face.

In equal parts, she loved and hated how much he cared, and suddenly all the pleasure went out of taunting him. "Why do you have to be so adorable?" she blurted. "Okay, I'll explain, but I'm leaving in the morning." With her mind made up, she straightened her spine. No more people would die because of her.

"Not happening. Now talk. No fairy tales. I don't want to fight, sweetheart." Winter stroked her cheek.

"Me either," she agreed, biting back tears.

"Damn, I'm sorry. I shouldn't have yelled."

They rubbed noses and the warmth of his breath caressed her mouth. "It's me who needs to apologize. Thank you. For being worried." She sighed and wondered if she should just settle for one heck of a goodbye kiss. Letting Winter in could end up being the biggest mistake of her life, but it was time to stop running. *Here goes everything.* Deep breath.

"Five years ago, my best friend Josie and I finished our senior college year and wanted to do something special to celebrate. My brother Steve worked at one of Boston's A-lister clubs, and he arranged a pass for the night."

"What kind of club? Where?" Winter asked.

"Twilight, in Boston. Dancing, drinking." Seriously, he might be older, but what did he imagine? Maggie rolled her eyes. "Please don't interrupt or I'll never finish."

"Sorry, go ahead."

Inching closer, he raised their interlaced fingers to his chest. Wishing she had a speck of his courage, she settled for the inviting pulse of Winter's heart against her skin. His musky male scent invaded her nostrils, and she couldn't resist pecking his cheek.

"After a couple of hours, we, make that me, tired of the constant thump of the music. I'm never great in crowds." Winter stroked her ear. "No, my hearing used to be twenty-twenty. Oh, that's the eyes, right? Never mind." Damn, she wanted to hug him.

A quick swipe of the tear pricking the corner of her eye set her back on track. "One too many tequilas later we were both a little drunk, and Josie felt sick. Urgently needing fresh air, we made a run for the fire exit and sat in the doorway while she heaved. I remember being angry at myself for partying because I still had an internship application to finish, but we'd been promising to go for ages. I cursed Josie out for being a pain. Not proud of that." Maggie coughed, but nothing cleared the guilt lodged in her throat.

"Take your time. I'm not going anywhere." Winter's eyes searched her face, patiently waiting for her to pull her act together.

"We were out back in the alley, and I was going to call a cab when I spotted Steve under the fire escape. On a break, smoking a cigarette. I thought, great, he'll find us a ride home. Thanks to the tequila, my legs weren't cooperating, so it took me a minute to get myself off the ground. That's when I saw him. Another man at the entrance to the alley, pointing what looked like a gun at Steve."

Air whistled under the closed door, swirling around her ankles, as though her brother were right there with them. *Keep going, sis. You got this.*

"Steve yelled for us to get out of there, and I tried to lift Josie, but she was too heavy. The guy was running down the alley and I panicked."

Maggie's heart hammered. No air. She wrenched her hand from Winter's and clutched her throat. "Oh God."

"Easy. With me. Breathe in, out. That's it."

Winter's firm grasp on her shoulders was the only thing keeping her from passing out. She sucked in oxygen as though the universe had run out and didn't expect a delivery soon. It took a few tries, but her heart rate slowed, and the room stopped spinning. Winter ran his hands along her thighs, grounding her. *Safe.* His touch spoke much louder than any words.

"There was nothing I could do. The man shot Steve." Her tone was flat, because it was the only way she could say the words without completely losing it. "Josie screamed, kept on screaming. I'll never stop hearing him shouting at her, 'quiet bitch', right before he shot her, too. Just because she wouldn't stop freaking out."

Maggie buried her face in Winter's chest and pressed her hands against her ears until it hurt. If she couldn't see the picture is her head, couldn't hear her friend scream, it must be a dream. How many times had she wished that over the years?

Winter caressed her hair. Long, uninterrupted strokes and whispered, "I've got you, Maggie. I swear, you are not alone."

Feeling stronger, she turned her cheek and looked at him. "I froze, positive I was next. The last thing I remember was their murderer hitting me hard across the side of my head. When I woke up in the hospital, doctors, nurses, were talking to me, but they sounded as though they were under the blanket. They couldn't do anything. I lost the hearing in my right ear. Why didn't Lazenby kill me? I should be dead, too."

"I'm sorry, sweetheart." His words rustled against her ear.

"It took a month, but they caught him. Frank Lazenby. I gave evidence at his trial. Stupid, stupid. An argument over a drink. He was drunk, and Steve refused to serve him."

Maggie wished herself light years away—living another life. A life filled with normal where Winter taught her to fish before they headed home to watch a movie or read a book by the fire before they ordered pizza, and they ended every day, lost in each other's arms.

Right now, all she offered Winter were tears and a soggy

shirt. "That night, when you found me sleeping in the park, a detective involved in Steve's case called. Told me Lazenby had escaped.

"Hell. Why didn't you say something?"

Certain he meant to pull away, she latched onto Winter's wrists. "Please don't be mad."

"Dammit. I'm not. Not at you. At myself for not being that man, the one you could ask for help. Maggie…"

"Shh. You are, Winter. Steve's dead. Nothing can change that, and it's time Lazenby burned in hell. Yesterday, I found this in the mailbox." She took the note out of her pocket and handed it to him. When he didn't say anything right away, she kept going. "He also left these. They went missing that night."

Winter's large hand curled around her much smaller one. "I'm so sorry. I knew something wasn't right, and intended to find out what was wrong after the meeting, but I shouldn't have waited. This." He shook the note. "I wish you'd made me stop, told me. Not kept everything bottled up inside you."

"It's not your problem."

Strong fingers curled tighter around her fist. "You're confusing shit, sweetheart. You are not the problem, but this threat is serious."

"Will you help me?" Immediately, she regretted saying anything. Asking for help was never easy. Afraid Winter would hate her for asking, or worse, take her up on her request, she traced his lips with her finger. "Forget I asked. The police will find him."

Things were escalating quickly, and she wasn't sure that dragging Winter into this was such a great idea. Seeing him hurt, possibly killed, because of her was the last thing she wanted. Rising from the couch, she stood by the fire and drank in the amazing man sitting opposite. "Phew. Now that's off my chest, I would love an enormous glass of something hugely alcoholic. Neat."

CHAPTER
THIRTY-ONE

"YOU DON'T HAVE to ask. Lazenby will never hurt you again. One way or another, the murdering fuck is a dead man." Winter packed enough menace behind his words to make sure Maggie understood.

"And, for the record, I will never forget anything you say or do. Everything about you is important to me. And you won't need alcohol to feel better." Two strides and he stood in front of her, his hand soaring to its favorite place, his palm cupping the back of her neck as he pulled her closer. "Got it?"

"Thanks." The tip of her tongue swept across her bottom lip.

He counted the seconds before he could kiss her without overwhelming her. Enraged by the horror of what Maggie had endured, he didn't think he could be gentle, that he could control how compelled he was to protect her, prevent her any more pain. Maggie thought she had weird ideas. If she walked in his shoes for a few breaths, she'd run, and this time he wasn't sure he'd stop her.

"I hate it when your face crinkles like used toilet paper."

Surprise! "Graphic." Winter chuckled.

Frustrated fingers tugged his shirt. "The police will find him. If you don't want that beer, is it all right if I make you smile again, my way?" She nudged him backwards.

"You must know it is, sweetheart." His calves hit the couch, and he grabbed Maggie's elbow and steadied her. Lying on her back, looking up at him, his fucking willpower took the jet plane to elsewhere. Winter pressed his tongue against her sweet lips and prayed she'd let him into her warm, wet mouth. When she opened a fraction to sigh, he dived right in, pulling away for a fraction of a second to grow. "Or we could have that drink."

"Hah! No siree. *Young* people have itsy-bitsy attention spans." Maggie grinned, her mouth bumping against his, and hooked her arms over his head.

His mind raced with all the things he'd like to do to her, starting with hauling her to her feet and pinning her against the wall. Hands aching to carry out the plan needed a distraction. They slid over her thighs and snatched the hem of her shirt.

The catch in her breath, the squirm of her pelvis sweeping shallow circles around his cock. *Fuck!* Winter widened the space between them. He had stuff to tell her before they took this much, much further.

"Something wrong?" she asked, running her fingers through his hair.

"No." He angled his body, slipped his knee onto the couch, and braced his weight on his hand.

"Hey. You are scaring the bejeebers out of me. Newsflash

—we are way beyond pathetic moments. Don't tell me you have a wife," she groaned. "Or have weeks to live. Damn. You're not dying, are you?"

"Hell, no." His voice rose a couple of octaves, blown away by how fucking far Maggie's mind traveled in sixty seconds and how alive he felt just looking at her blue eyes rocking the possibilities. "I'm leaving," he blurted. No point figuring out an easier way to tell her. Then he held his breath.

She smiled. Not the reaction he expected. He blinked because wanting her in his home, on a more than a temporary basis, was an idea he'd kinda enjoyed getting used to.

Untraveled territory minus a map, a plan. Never his thing until Maggie. "I'm not sure when. Snake is waiting on the final okay, but within the next couple of days. But after what you told me, I'll ask Snake to send a replacement. No way am I leaving you here alone without me."

"I see." Her hand twitched nervously as though it meant to push him away the exact same time as her smile said come here. "But I can't let you do that. Sentinel is more than a job for you, and it's not like we're in an actual relationship or anything. You won't always be here to look after me. Snake can arrange security until they find Lazenby, right? Great. Go. Enjoy." She chuckled. "Oh, Winter, stop frowning. Just come back safe."

Whoever ruled the world, god or gremlin, had fucked up notions on timing. For instance, take this moment. The one where he wanted to tell her he'd fallen hook, line, and sinker, that he needed her in his life and that moving a mountain, clearing the Brooklyn Bridge of traffic, was not a problem. Anything just so she understood how much he lov…

"It won't be for long. Sam will be alone, too. I'm sure she won't mind if I stay with her while I look for an apartment. Bad ass ex-military, she can take down Lazenby if he shows, so there's no need to worry."

The hairs on his arms bristled. *I love you.* The words hung in the if and maybe strung between them, but when he told her, he wanted to do it right. Special, with at least three days to show her.

She knew who he was, what he did. She'd seen him work up close in Pakistan. There would always be another job. Short notice, indefinite schedule.

It had gotten dark outside. Maggie sat up and rubbed her eye. He pulled back off his knee and reached behind him to turn on the lamp sitting on the small table. "Better?" He had a strong feeling her answer was no, and that his heart was breaking because of it.

"Do you have a family?" she asked.

Knowing he'd said all the wrong stuff, but not sure how to fix it, he laid his palm on her knee and followed her lead.

"Only child. Good thing. My folks weren't great at parenting. Should have divorced, but never did. Then mom died. Haven't seen her husband since the day I enlisted. Sentinel's the only family I need. Snake, Storm, Trig, Havoc, even the new guy, Mowgli, we have each other's backs. I'd take a bullet for them. They'd do the same for me. Short of climbing into bed with each other, not sure how we could be any closer."

Winter forced a laugh. A fucking lame attempt at lifting the doom blanket tenting over their heads.

"I'm sorry. That must be tough. Not knowing where your father is." Maggie gave a word to the cocksucker he didn't deserve. "If he's still alive."

The tip of her pinkie shaved the back of his hand. Blind-sided by her insight, concern, but most of all the sadness lacing her voice, Winter strained to hear the knock at the door he knew wouldn't come until morning, but half-hoped would happen early and let him off the hook.

"Sorry. I didn't mean to upset you. All this heavy talk. Sucks. I'll go pack up my stuff and call Sam. If the offer still stands, I would love that drink." Maggie stood.

Winter snatched her wrist and pulled her back beside him. "Damn it. How many times do you need to hear it? You have nothing to be sorry for. Given everything that has happened, you amaze me. You're strong, caring and the most patient person I ever met. Look how you handle me. You're the only woman who dares to put up with toilet face." He unclenched her fist and kissed her palm.

Fuck knew how long they sat like love-sick teenagers, holding hands, staring at the wall, before Maggie spoke.

"Winter?"

"Uh-huh." He waited.

"Take me to bed."

"Thought you'd never ask." Light as a breath of fresh air, in one move, he lifted her into his arms.

"Show off," she squeaked.

He winked. Judging by the giggle flying past his ear, the woman was impressed.

Moving as fast as he safely dared, he raced down the stairs to his room and tossed her onto the mattress. Christ, he wanted her naked. Now. While Maggie recovered from the laugh that rocked and bounced her lithe body, he pulled his shirt over his head. His belt gone, and the button on his pants undone, before she scrambled to the edge of the bed, dragged down his zipper and cupped his erection.

"Hell, sweetheart," he gulped and shoved his jocks and jeans to his knees.

"I've been dying to do this, Winter. Please tell me you like head." Sitting back on her heels, she licked her perfect lips.

The hand fisting her hair shook with the control it took to stay still. He focused on his cock, the end purple with need, crying out for her mouth to suck him. Almost lost it when she rose up to take off her top and unclip her bra. Her breasts weren't big, but they were perfectly round with pale pink peaks begging to be sucked.

Maggie leaned forward. His legs trembled. Precum oozed from the top of his shaft and when a spray curl fell in front of her face he brushed it behind her ear. He didn't want to miss the sight of her tongue licking him from base to tip.

"You're sure this is okay," she hummed. Her pretty pink fingernails raking his inside thighs.

"Do it, sweetheart," he rasped and pressed her head to his cock.

Slowly her head bobbed up and down, her mouth taking a bit more of him each time until he thought he'd explode. Maggie's wasn't the most experienced, but the sensation of her teeth scraping his sensitive flesh was mind-blowingly erotic.

"You taste amazing."

He loved her growly groan. Tightening his grip on her

hair, he urged her to move faster. Unbelievable. His cock nudged the back of her throat. Maggie swallowed and the tight pressure she had on him made him see fucking stars.

Each stroke of the delicate hand wrapped tightly around the base brought him closer to his release. "So good, sweetheart." But he needed more, needed to fuck her until she begged him to make her come.

"Christ!" She squeezed his balls and pleasure-pain shot from his tailbone to his throat, robbing him of his next breath and wiping his mind of so much shit he couldn't stop the tear rolling down his cheek. He seized Maggie's thighs and flipped her onto her back, ignored her yelp and dragged her jeans and panties along her slim legs and onto the floor.

"Lie still," Winter ordered. No way would he come without making sure she did first.

He grabbed a condom from the drawer of the bedside table, rolled it over his cock, and thrust inside her. Withdrew then sank deeper, cursing out loud as he drowned in her wet heat.

Maggie lifted her head and ran the tip of her tongue over his nipple, bit him hard.

"I want you so much, my clit feels like it's on fire."

"Jesus, woman. I said, lie still." Her words alone were enough to drive him over the edge.

Her gaze blazed through him, slicing his heart into a million fucking pieces, each of them wanting her more than the next. In his bed, in his life. "Turn over." He reached underneath her and helped her flip. "On your knees, hands on the wall."

Every one of Maggie's groans upped his blood pressure

until he couldn't see straight. His jaw tightened as he fought to hold back when all he wanted to do was bury himself inside her. "I don't want to hurt you, sweetheart. But..."

"For the love of heaven, Winter. Fuck me."

CHAPTER
THIRTY-TWO

EVERYTHING HAD a place in the order-obsessed man's life and Winter's fridge was no exception. Awestruck Maggie hunched over the open door, marvelling at the tiers of Glasslock containers stacked on top of one another. The neatly arranged, according to height, bottles in the rack. He bought the best when it came to organizing his food. It went without saying that leftovers were nowhere in sight.

Way too early in the morning for tampering with the system, but she checked for cream. There wasn't any. Stifling an enormous yawn, she closed the door. Arms waving in front of her, she staggered for the ever-faithful coffeemaker, disappointed Winter had left for work without saying goodbye.

Being a sweetheart, he probably didn't want to wake her. No note either. Okay, she got that, too. The stormy look on his face when she showed him Lazenby's note had softened briefly, only to morph into genuine regret at her pain. Maybe he thought that finding a piece of paper next to her pillow when she was half awake could be a trigger. But no text?

And that could have made sense on any other day, stopped her obsessing, if the image of Winter's furrowed brow when he came refused to fade from her memory. The way he shouted her name as his climax shook him rang in her deaf ear.

Flowers would have been great. She thumped the kitchen bench, disgusted at the impossible hoops she believed Winter should jump through. The blow reverberating along her forearm and tingling her fingertips made her feel strong, grounded. Stop her over thinking stuff. Already she missed Winter, wanted him back. Not in twenty-four hours, a week, a month. Heck, he'd said he didn't know when he'd return.

Last night, he'd flipped her onto her knees and made love to her from behind. She'd never done that before and not been able to look at him was unsettling. At first, until she lost herself in the sound and smell of how good they were together, and she matched his power and rhythm as best she knew how. Listened to the rush of her breathing as Winter explored her body and drove her soul to unexplored places.

She flopped onto the bar stool, her stomach in knots. Coffee without cream didn't sound appealing, so she took a huge breath and tried not to give into the nagging doubt. What if he never came back? Or what if he did, convinced she was fine staying with Sam and Snake and it was the perfect time to reclaim his space?

The fridge door beeped, mad at her for leaving it open. "Okay, okay." Sam would arrive soon, and thanks to Winter deliciously messing with her plans last night, she still had to pack. She kicked the door closed, went searching for her hearing aid, and decided to send him a message. But *have a good day* didn't seem appropriate.

After a shower and dressing in breakneck speed, she made sure her aid was secure and stared at the few girlie toiletries she'd accumulated over the past few weeks.

Take them all. The serious face staring at her from the bathroom mirror insisted. Thankfully, the intercom blared before she spun down the lack of confidence path again.

Grabbing her bag off the bed, she gulped the last of the cold, black coffee, switched off the lights and hurried to the door.

"Hey, girl. What took you the fuck so long?"

"Morning, Sam. Sleep well?"

"Nope. Never do, the night before Snake takes off on a job. You?" Sam asked as they jogged down the steps.

Her usual in-your-face honesty caught the piece of Maggie she'd been shoving away since she woke up alone next to Winter's stone cold side of the bed. "Oh, Sam." The tears rolled down her cheek.

"I got ya. Life without our alpha dogs sucks." Sam slung her arm around Maggie's shoulders. "But come on, thank God it's Friday and all that crap. We have shopping to do."

"Shopping?" Sam hadn't mentioned it last night when she'd called to ask for a place to stay.

"Yeah, the girls are coming over for a sleepover and we're in charge of snacks. Extras for the boof head body-guards Snake has posted. Although they won't get a sniff of the copious amounts of alcohol."

"Sounds great." Sam threw her arms around her, and they stood on the sidewalk hugging each other for a moment before Maggie turned to set the alarm. Door firmly and securely shut, they headed to Sam's truck.

She fastened her seatbelt and wiped what she promised

herself was her last tear from her eye, even if her heart still felt like a lead lollipop in her chest.

Sam smiled and squeezed her hand before driving away. Winter insisted his teammates were his brothers, his family, and suddenly she understood. Together, they'd get through the next, however long. No use making up stories about what might happen. Live in the moment and take it like a woman. She flashed Sam a grin.

"Thatta girl. How about you and I indulge in an express mani-pedi before we shop?"

Pedicures made her squirm, but the toe-curling upgrade was exactly what she needed to take her mind off Winter. Maggie leaned forward and adjusted the music volume. Upbeat. No sad, on-my-own song, blaring through the speakers—not cool.

"Agree? Trip to the salon?" Sam nudged her elbow.

"Perfect."

For once, traffic wasn't too bad, and when they finally arrived at Sam's place, the others were already there. Winter had assured her she'd be safe there, so she didn't ask how. Jenna must have a key. As they drove through the gate at the end of the long drive up to the house, Sam had pointed out one of the Sentinel bodyguards keeping watch in the trees.

Sure enough, Jenna came out to meet them as soon as they pulled up. "Grab your stuff from the boot, and come inside," Sam said as she hugged her friend.

Boot? Trunk. Maggie didn't say it aloud, but Sam's Brit words always made her grin. She looked forward to learning more of them over the next… Her heart sank.

"You feeling okay, Maggie? No aftereffects from your

bump on the head. You're looking pale." Jenna asked, dragging her back to the present.

"No, I'm fine. Blame Sam's mad driving." She winked at Jenna and grabbed her bag.

"Oh, you will pay, Miss King. You get to peel potatoes. Boss' orders."

"I deserved that. Punishment accepted." Laughing nervously, Maggie went back to grab the jacket she'd left on her seat. She was looking forward to the evening, dying to ask Sam how she kept it together when Snake was away.

The others had gone inside, but same as before, Linda blocked the doorway. What was it with this woman?

"Hi, I'm Mia." A woman's head peered over Linda's shoulder. "Shove over, Linda. Let Maggie pass."

Another Brit. Things were looking up. This slumber party had potential. An opportunity to push away all her Winter insecurities. Have fun because she sure as hell hated being miserable. Lazenby on the loose didn't help, but she refused to let him win. Pulling her shoulders back, she sailed past Linda, determined not to spoil everyone's night with a long face and crap attitude.

Two hours later, they were sitting around the fire in Sam's huge open plan living area. Head on their paws, George and Bounce huddled together at Maggie's feet. Stuffed to the eyeballs with fried chicken and pizza, she groaned.

"What was that? You can't manage any waffles and ice cream? Isn't it a national dish? I made it especially." Jenna sniffed a couple of times and swiped a fake tear from her cheek.

"Sure is," Linda said, grabbing a bowl and shoving it

under Maggie's nose. "What's the matter? Scared of getting fatter?"

"Ouch. No more wine for you." Sam reached for the bottle of Pino Grigio clutched in Linda's hand.

She'd been nursing it, that and the one before, ever since they started making dinner. Maggie knew Linda didn't mean what she'd said. It had to be a joke, even if she didn't feel much like laughing. She was most definitely not overweight. Winter was always trying to get her to eat more. No, Linda had a whacked sense of humor, but why must Sentinel's receptionist take every opportunity to pick on her?

"Come on, Linda. Give." Sam snatched the bottle of wine from her grasp and whisked it away.

Maggie laughed out loud when she saw the label. *The Naked Grape.*

Jenna nudged her elbow. "I know who I'd like to get naked, and his name isn't Grape," she said.

"What? Who?" Mia exclaimed.

All eyes fixed on Jenna. A little older than the rest, Maggie thought of her as the quiet one. Being a doc, she assumed she was also the most sensible. Looking at her, hugging herself, eyes rolling to the ceiling, cute dimples hollowing her cheeks, she might have got that wrong.

"Girl. You cannot leave that statement hanging there," Linda groaned.

For once, Maggie agreed with her.

"Spill the fuck right now." Sam perched on the arm of Jenna's chair and pinched her friend.

"There's nothing to spill. I'm not even sure he feels the same, but I'm hoping he might. He's so..." Her voice trailed off and a collective moan circled the room.

"Who?" Maggie asked, secretly hoping it wasn't Winter, which was insane considering he hadn't left her side since he found her in the park.

"Okay, okay. Storm. He's gorgeous and Tom adores him. You know how my lad can be, Sam?"

"I do. Kids, especially teenagers, are difficult. You are a remarkable mum, and you should be proud. Not sure I'd have your strength." Sam kissed the top of her friend's head.

Maggie swirled the wine in her glass.

"Tom's not that bad. Normal, the best part of my life. If anything ever happened to him, I wouldn't survive."

The last time they had all been together, it was obvious Jenna hadn't stopped grieving for her dead husband. Maggie could relate. Her heart went out to her and Tom. Unexpectedly losing those you loved left a dead part low in the gut that nothing could fill.

"Lighten up. Did anyone say chocolate?" Jenna leapt out of her chair. Maggie couldn't help but feel that the hand clutching the front of her wrap held more together than the silky material.

"I need another drink." Linda grumbled.

During the last hour, the wind had picked up, blowing across the property, and finding its way through the gaps into the house. "Anyone mind?" Seemed polite to ask as Maggie grabbed the sheepskin throw.

"Knock yourself out." Sam flopped into Jenna's chair, reached behind her head, and tossed her a pillow. "Make yourself comfy."

"I'd love to have a child, one day. And trust me, it better be a boy, because Havoc would never let a daughter out of his sight." Mia giggled, but Maggie didn't miss the trail off in her tone.

Being partially deaf meant she had to work hard to catch stuff that sailed over most people's heads. *One day.* She couldn't help wondering. Havoc's adopted son, Charlie, was a handful, they adored, but they both had careers.

"Not for me." Linda called out from the kitchen.

When she walked back into the main room, glass full, carrying a full bottle of wine, Maggie sighed.

"I can't imagine why anyone wants kids. Smelly, noisy, always wanting attention."

"Not like anyone we know." Sam added.

Maggie stifled a snort. "I've always wanted a family. Three, make that four, children. Two of each."

"Not planning on that with Winter, I hope." Linda said.

Maggie flushed. "I wasn't thinking of anyone in particular."

"Good, because he's not your man. Take it from me. We dated."

Maggie gulped. "Oh. When?"

"Not long before you arrived. Apparently, it's a thing with him, bed the new girl, then ghost her."

Maggie sniffed and wished she had a glass of whatever Linda was drinking.

"Oh, no. Don't tell me you fell for his shit? Anyway, aren't you scared you'll pass on your, you know?" She tugged her ear. "Your disability."

Maggie struggled to speak. Tears clogging the back of her throat. "My hearing… deafness… it's not genetic."

"Oh. Kay. I'm going to find chocolate." Jenna said. "Want to help me, Maggie?"

"Great idea. Put on a large pot of coffee while you're there. Some of us need it more than others." Sam glared at Linda.

"I think I'll go to bed." Rattled and more than a little angry with Linda, an early night would do her good, stop her from saying something she'd regret in the morning. Winter didn't have to mention he'd dated Linda, but it would have been nice to know. If nothing else, it made sense why she was constantly in her sights.

If fact, Linda may be her BFF, saving her from making more of a fool of herself with him than she already had. No girl wanted to be a guy's trophy bed mate. She cringed. Hah! Every negative had a positive. Any new boyfriend had a high benchmark to top. The hook Linda had dug under her breastbone hurt like hell. She couldn't get out of there fast enough, but her foot caught the edge of the coffee table and she stumbled. Fortunately, Sam caught her elbow before she fell.

"Steady. Come on. My bed is calling too," she said. "'Night, ladies. Leave the washing up, I'll do it in the morning. Said no one ever."

Maggie appreciated Sam's half smile, but completely failed to flip it back.

"Don't let her get to you. Linda's a bitch. If it weren't for Mia's soft heart, we'd have dumped her arse weeks ago."

Maggie stood outside her room, desperately needing to be alone. "Is it that obvious?"

"Is that a real question, love?" Sam's hand hung off Maggie's shoulder. "Look, I'm not pretending I know what went down with Winter and Linda, but trust me, despite what she says about him."

"You mean, drop dead gorgeous, can have any gal he wants?"

"Stop. I was going to say, he's not the kind of man who leads any woman where they don't want to go. And…"

A door squeaked. Afraid someone would hear them talking, Maggie gave her full weight to her hip, turned the knob and shoved open her door. "Good night. Thanks for letting me stay."

"No problem. Winter will have my head if I let anything happen to you. Sleep tight. Sweet dreams."

This time, Maggie matched Sam's wry smile. Too tired to undress, she grabbed the extra pillow from the end of the bed and slipped under the comforter. Her cold feet would be a heck of a lot warmer snuggled under Winter's thigh. She rubbed her toes together and tucked her hands under her chin and felt guilty for letting Linda get to her.

One hundred, ninety-nine, ninety eight. Maggie began the sleep countdown, bit her bottom lip, and drifted off, vowing to work on her trust issues.

CHAPTER
THIRTY-THREE

ON YOUR TOES meant facing every mission able to shift, at speed, to unexpected threats. Ready for Plan A, B, most definitely fucking C, to turn to dust often before the plane had landed. No fucking surprise when that's exactly what happened.

The final plan, the only one worth a fuck, crammed into everyone's brain as they carried out last minute checks before the halo drop into Burkina.

Three days later, thanks to Knight, head of Sentinel Security in London and his on the ground contact, they were within five clicks of where six American businessmen were being held captive in the African Sahel.

Mission objective. Rescue the hostages and execute immediate exfil. Head on a swivel, Winter scoped their surroundings, a token exercise, nothing more. No excellent cover trees had sprouted in the last ten minutes. The sun hadn't met a cloud in months. Sitting ducks. They should be quacking.

Silently, Winter's team concentrated on the only rule that mattered. *Stay the fuck alive and come home.*

Four or five men huddled in a group outside a shack cobbled together from wood and metal and chunks of concrete. A couple of kids were kicking a football.

Storm's heavy sigh blew through Winter's earpiece. Yep. Everyone hated adding children to the mix, dreaded the day innocents became collateral damage. Early in the piece, when he'd joined the military, Winter had accepted if that ever happened to him and he killed a child, his life would be over. Time to hang up his shit forever. The kid's ball landed at his feet.

"Keep moving," Snake ordered. His tone laced with warning.

"Yeah, yeah," Winter hissed as Maggie's face slid into focus. Peacefully sleeping when he left, most of it covered by her long, blond hair. He'd stayed a few seconds longer than he should have listening to her snuffles, wishing to hell he didn't have to leave, but he hadn't had the heart to wake her.

Truth, he was worried she'd blast him for being too rough. Bragging aside, his cock matched his size. A big man who had pounded into her as if his life depended upon it. Hearing her say that he'd hurt her would have broken him.

"Three o'clock," Storm said.

"I see it." Snake acknowledged.

The house was like any other, except for the two men standing either side of the door, AK47s hanging off their shoulders, like hairs on a catwalk model.

"Keep moving." Snake slowed his pace, indicated they back off, but progress.

After the boss checked to see no one was paying him

particular attention, he signalled him and Trig to head right of the entrance, as Havoc and Storm joined from the left.

Winter offered a barely perceptible chin lift to Trig. In tandem, they angled their feet toward their destination. Unease bubbled in his gut. The surrounding air, filled with their collective held breath, grew thicker the closer they got to the hut, along with the shit sure feeling the devil had finally woken up.

A flick of Trig's hand was their signal. Nothing much, but for a team attuned to each other as they were it was enough. *Three, two, one.* In his head, Winter counted down the seconds. Snake and Havoc pulled their concealed weapons from underneath their tunics and butted the guards in the head. Crumpled on the floor, one dick raised his weapon before both received a tap to the chest that kept them down for good.

Winter didn't have to look to know Trig cover his six as they followed their teammates into the hut. The fucking shit hole stank. A huge bucket in the corner, proof. The hair on the back of his neck stood to attention. He trained his weapon on the open door and waited for the guys across the street to storm in behind them.

Breath he'd been holding whooshed from his lungs dispersed with the same speed of the bullet he despatched into the chest of the guy running at him, knife raised.

The black cloud hanging above them tore wide open from the shrieks of the rescued hostages. His weapon still trained on the door, Winter stepped back a few paces and used his free hand to help untie the prisoners. They were naked, their clothes tossed around them. "Don't touch," he snapped as one guy grabbed his arm. Harsh, but this wasn't over, not nearly.

"Hurry. Get dressed." Trigger said as he and Havoc gathered up the clothes from the floor and randomly tossed them at the group.

Snake gave them another couple of seconds to find shoes that fit before they corralled everyone into the daylight. Immediately, hands flew to their eyes. Cooped up inside hadn't been easy for the hostages, but they couldn't risk waiting for them to adjust.

The boy who'd been kicking the ball made a dash for him, crashing into his thigh. Light as a feather, Winter hardly felt the blow. Too skinny, too young to be a witness to this clusterfuck. *"Laisse-le tranquille."* Leave him alone, Snake commanded.

Winter reached into his pocket and pulled the last of the candy he always kept there. Something sweet for long nights when sour memories refused to let him sleep. He thought of Maggie and her fucking passion for soggy chocolate chip cookies. What was she doing now? Snake had checked with Sam a few hours ago, and she'd assured him they were all safe. No sign of Lazenby.

"Prends les bonbons. Take the candy." Winter's fingers flicked over the boy's retreating head. Crazy. He knew better.

"What the fuck?" Storm hissed.

His buddy swung him away from the kid and back to the hostages shuffling out of the village. No one followed. Another day in fucking paradise as they returned to getting on with lives too often interrupted by Mali terrorists.

CHAPTER
THIRTY-FOUR

FIVE DAYS Later

Winter must be the only person here that didn't rate McNamara's, but the Irish bar ranked high on the boss' fave Manhattan watering holes, so here they were. He and his team sat on a line of stools facing the huge hundred-year-old mirror. The smell of stale Guinness surrounding them. Waiting.

"Drink your beer, man. You're twitchy as a bird in a cattery. Maggie will be here." Trigger waved his index finger at the bartender, who deposited a full Heineken next to the half-drunk bottle Winter had started an hour ago.

"You heard from Sam? Winter leaned his elbows on the bar and tossed the question along two stools to Snake. Mowgli had assumed guard duty for the night and was bringing the women into the city.

"They're late," the boss replied, taking another long swig from the schooner of larger he favored. "Traffic. It's busier than Piccadilly Circus out there." Snake scrubbed the back of his neck.

No shit! Winter shook his head and nudged the unopened Heineken along the bar to Storm. Place was turning into a damn Sushi Train.

Time, the fucker, had been marching at a snail's pace since they left Burkina. Ticking his life away one millisecond at a time, but it had given him space. He hesitated to call it the breathing kind to prepare—get his words right. Vowels and consonants were all in a row, except what came out of his mouth when Maggie's fine ass finally waltzed through the door was anyone's guess.

If, by some miracle, she wanted to see him half as much as he couldn't wait to lose himself in her smile, they'd be in his truck and heading home to Brooklyn before she could order a lemonade.

"I'll say this. What that woman lacks in admin skills, she certainly makes up for on the dance floor." Trigger groaned.

"What the fuck?" Winter turned and looked along the line of Trigger's gaze.

"Tenshun! Incoming."

Sure enough, Linda, elbows bent, seaweed arms waving above her head, swayed toward them. No man in his right fucking mind wouldn't appreciate the woman's curves. Her body just didn't turn him on. Didn't compare to Maggie King. The weight of her perfect breasts in his hands, the silky softness of her skin.

"Winter," Linda breathed, crooking her finger at him. *Come to me*, written all over her face.

"Oh man. Some guys have all the luck." Storm chuckled, kicking Winter's chair with the toe of his boot.

Before he could make it to the head, Linda stood in front

of him, her hands pinned to the bar on either side of his shoulders. Her bottom lip curled. Ample cleavage pouring over her low-cut T-shirt.

"Linda. How's it going?" Christ. That sounded lame. He kicked himself for not having *that* talk weeks earlier and wasn't about to be rude. But if that's what it took to have her understand he had zero interest, perhaps tonight was the night.

"All the better for seeing you, Winter. Glad you're back safe and looking mighty fine."

Trigger cleared his throat.

You see what I'm up against, here? He beamed the words at his bud, begging him to come to the rescue, but the dickhead was having far too much fun.

"Dance with me, Winter. I've been a lonely girl with you gone." She purred, low and too fucking intimate, like he was the only person sitting in McNamara's.

"Sorry, sugar. I don't dance."

"Bullshit." Storm joined the act.

Sure as shit, he was going to strangle his brothers as soon as he got rid of Linda. He grabbed her wrists and gently eased them off the bar. "'Scuse me. Nature calls."

"Oh, come on, Winter. One dance." She grabbed his belt and yanked him forward.

Her breath smelled of whiskey and if the way she rocked on her feet offered a clue if he moved too fast, she'd be flat on her ass. As much as he wanted her out of his space, he wouldn't hurt her or embarrass her. By his count, the woman had that covered.

Leaning back slightly, he caught her wrists in one hand,

placed the other around her waist to steady her, and was about to stand when her lips smacked his mouth with a grunt.

Too late, he looked to his brother for help as Maggie walked through the door.

Afraid he'd hurt Linda if he pushed the very drunk female plastered all over him, he turned to Trigger. "A little help here."

Trig nodded and raised his chin at Maggie, pushing through tables to get to the door. "Come on, babe. Let's get you home."

Trigger took Linda's arm, and Winter shot off his stool. "Wait," he called after her, but she didn't hear him or didn't care. Either way, she kept right on walking.

"What the hell, Winter?" Sam stepped in front of him.

"Hell nothing. She doesn't understand."

"Maybe. But she's in no mind to listen. I'll go. Stay here."

"Stand down, Winter." Snake grabbed his arm as his wife took off after Maggie.

"Get your hand off of me," he snarled. Boss or no boss. Maggie was not walking away. Not now. Never again if he could convince her to stay. Snake's jaw set at a don't-fuck-with-me angle, and he tightened his grip.

Why? Why did she, the best thing that had ever happened to him, arrive at that moment? Winter didn't hear his bellow bouncing off the walls of MacNamara's until every eye focused on the lunatic ripping his arm from Snake's hold and charging for the door. He made it to Sam as she opened it and they dashed onto the street.

Winter didn't need to see. He sensed his teammates

covering his six. "Stay back," he yelled at Sam. He should have known a trained military woman like her would keep right on coming.

Rain had turned to sleet in the past hour, but the wet shards slashing across his face had fuck all to do with the ice blood in his veins. Maggie screamed. A bald guy held her legs as another in the black hoodie grabbed her under the armpits and forced her into a van.

Kicking and screaming, his woman fought like hell to stop them from succeeding, buying him time to reach for the weapon in the hip holster under his jacket.

All he cared about was getting to her, fast, before they drove away. No one fucked with Maggie and got away with it. All four of them were trained to rescue hostages. Slowly, he eased forward. With each breath, the tension building inside every fiber of his body found a place to settle. All he needed was one clean shot.

In his peripheral vision, his teammates were fanning out, covering as much as the space between him and Maggie as possible. "Easy," he murmured as his free hand flew to the side, blocking his brothers. "Let her go, Lazenby." His stomach clenched. And what were the chances of that happening?

"I've got him," Storm said, and started to move ahead.

"No." A single word enough to make his friend stop and nod.

Grateful they acknowledged his lead, Winter bent down, put his weapon on the sidewalk, and raised his hand. "Let's talk. You're surrounded. No one's going anywhere. Let her go, if you want to live." His fear was getting the better of him. He took a breath trying to rein back in his control, but the sight of Maggie in that fucker's arms, the tears in eyes begging him to stay back, was shredding years of military training.

"I don't think so, asshole. You will stay exactly where you are if you don't want me to snap her pretty neck." Lazenby hollered.

"It will be okay, Winter. Please." Maggie gasped.

Lazenby tightened his grip. "Shut the fuck up."

Oh yeah, the fucker was losing it, and that was the moment Winter knew he had to take if he ever hoped to hold Maggie in his arms. In a flash, he dropped to one knee and pulled his second weapon from his ankle holster.

One breath to laser in on his target. Two shots to Lazenby's head and he collapsed into the blood already pooling at his feet. Maggie screamed.

No. Too late. The other guy bellowed and began punching her in the face. Winter ran, but she was on the ground, the man's boots crashing into her head.

Trembling so hard, he wasn't sure if he could stay upright long enough to reach her. He tried to call out, but his voice had gone AWOL, along with his mind.

On the run, he raised his gun again and blew the fucker away. His hands were shaking as he knelt beside Maggie and checked for a pulse. "She's alive," he called to his teammates. *Thank God.* He wanted to cradle her in his arms but wasn't sure how badly she was injured, so he took a moment to look her over while Storm took out his phone and called the paramedics.

"Winter?"

His heard skipped a few beats. "Yeah, sweetheart, it's me. You're safe."

She raised her hand and stroked his cheek, but immediately her eyes closed again and she went limp.

CHAPTER
THIRTY-FIVE

WINTER STOOD BY THE WINDOW, barely keeping it together while the doctor examined Maggie. After she had insisted he was family, under protest, the nursing staff had let him stay the night.

Stronger than anyone he had ever met, she didn't make a sound, but seeing her flinch every time the medic prodded and probed her fragile body drove him closer to the edge. Not wanting Maggie to suffer more pain, he was within striking distance of grabbing the doc's hands and pulling them off her.

"You are a lucky woman, Ms. King. Apart from a few cuts and bruises, there are no broken bones. No concussion. I will have one of the junior doctors suture the deeper cut on your arm, but it shouldn't require too many stitches."

Winter nodded. Remembering what Lazenby had threatened to do to Maggie if he hadn't stopped him, made him want to snatch the fucker's corpse out of the morgue and enjoy killing him all over again. But she didn't need his fury. She deserved his complete focus on helping her to heal. The wounds might be superficial, but she would want support and time to get over her ordeal. He intended being there for her if she'd have him.

"Thank you, doctor."

The quiet croak in her voice tore him apart. When he'd seen Lazenby's hands squeezing her throat, her body limp, eyes closed, he was sure he was too late, that the fucker had killed her.

"No problem, Ms. King. Now get some rest."

The doctor turned and left, and Maggie reached for him. Releasing the breath he didn't realise he'd been holding, Winter strode to the bed and took her hand. The zap of electricity shooting through their joined fingers awoke his guilt.

He brushed his lips across her forehead, choking with the memory of how he almost lost her. Life would not have been worth living.

"I'm so sorry." Staring at the bedcover, he swallowed long and hard, stifling the fear that threatened to end him.

"Winter. Look at me."

He dragged his gaze from the white waffle blanket and stared into her sea-blue eyes. Maggie could ask him to do anything. Hurl himself out of the window, and he'd jump headfirst. "Not sure I'll be able to take my eyes off you ever again."

"Sit here, next to me."

Winter did as she asked, went a step further. Kicked off his boots and raised his legs onto the bed.

"I have a question," she said before he could put his arm around her.

"Sure, sweetheart. What do you need? Water? Another blanket?"

"Shh. No. Well, my clothes would be good. Getting out of here, now, perfect, but before you go all growly bear on me, I realise that's unreasonable."

"Yes. Twenty-four hours, at least." If he had his way, it would be a week. Knowing how she loathed hospitals, it was important to reassure her. "Don't worry, you don't have to ask. I'm not leaving until you do. Trig's gone back to mine to fetch what I need."

"No, that's not my question."

He pulled her closer, tucked her head against his chest, and kissed her again. "What?"

"Linda? Are you two, you know, a thing? Because if you are, you've probably guessed I'm a one-man-at-a-time girl. And…"

He felt Maggie's tears. The growing damp patch on his shirt slew him. "What?" He snagged her chin and lifted her face so he could see what was messing with that head of hers.

"In the bar. I saw you." She sniffed.

"I know, and I'm sorry, but you must know Linda means zip to me. She'd had too much to drink and got pushy. That's all. I swear. There is nothing going on between me and that woman." Winter sucked in a breath, and willed Maggie to believe him.

"Good, I just wanted to make sure."

Relieved, he kept his mouth shut, didn't risk explaining, in case he messed up, and gently stroked the arm slung across his body. "'Night, sweet dreams."

CHAPTER
THIRTY-SIX

ONE MONTH Later

Lazenby would never bother her again, but Maggie didn't believe in closure. Forgetting her Steve and Josie wasn't something she wanted to do. Hopefully, with Winter's help, she could take tiny steps into the future.

Speakers sat high on the wall in every room in Winter's home, singing out a random loop of Coltrane and Nina. Right here, watching Winter concentrating so hard, that smoke puffed out of his ears and swirled through the house, she had never been happier.

He could shoot the pimple off flea's ass, but her bear had three left feet for dancing. Or it sure seemed like it. She'd seen him successfully put one foot behind the other many times. Ask him to do it in time with the music and it was as though an extra limb jumped in to help.

Her smile widened. "One, two, there. One, two, three." What had started out as a light tap of her shoe beating the rhythm had turned into a major thud. "Winter! Please tell me you can hear this beat." The one reverberating through every cell in her body. His massive frame swayed in a syncopated response that even in jazz's wildest incarnation never hit the on or the offbeat.

His eyebrows knitted together in a frown that said he had no idea what she meant. Snaking an arm behind her back, he pulled her in for the kiss that never failed to melt her bones. A sly grin curling the hairs of his day old stubble.

"Oh, no, big boy. I can read your mind. No nookies for you until you waltz me three times around this room. In time with the music." She added the last bit only so she could feel his groan rumble across her breasts. Love was in the little things.

"Nookies?" His smile lifted and caught a ride on the creases at the side of his eyes.

"Don't pretend you have no clue what I mean." Thumping him came to mind, but her fingers had other ideas and curled around his T-shirt. Difficult to get purchase, considering how the black material clung to his firm pecs. "Come on, Winter. Try. For me." She licked her top lip the way she proved many times crippled his control.

"For a squirt you sure play dirty." His nose nuzzled the side of her neck.

Her knees went weak. "Believe it. Oh, no. Are you pouting?" Who could resist running a finger across his pillowy bottom lip? Not her. His teeth gnashed, and the force of her laugh made her arch over the muscular arm glued to her lower back.

"Because if you did? You can kiss goodbye to your argument about our age difference being a major obstacle moving forward when you behave like a toddler." Leaning harder against his forearm, she looped her arms around his neck and closed her eyes.

Lifting her off her feet, Winter spun her in circles, and in a dizzy blur, she set her soul free to ride the melody swelling from the speakers. Surrounded by him, every bone, every muscle in her body said this was where she belonged. "I love you, Winter."

Winter stopped dead on the spot. Now she'd gone and done it. Said the one thing guaranteed to wreck the moment.

"Say it again," he growled in her ear.

Feet hovering off the ground, more than a little breathless, she clung to him as the room kept on spinning.

"That first day on the pier, inside…" Winter grabbed her curled fist and pressed it over his heart. "Deep down I knew I was hooked. A quiet afternoon fishing, until you caught me in your net, Maggie King. And I'll serve a lifetime sentence if you'll have me. Damn, I can't take my eyes off you. Say it again."

The tips of her toes hovered over the wooden floor. Desire for this amazing man took over, stirring her to press her pelvis against the bulge in the front of his pants. But it was so much more than sex with Winter. She cupped his face in her hands and kissed him. "I love you. There's lots more, but I can't find the words. Unbelievable? Pathetic, right?"

Winter chuckled. His head dipped low enough to pepper her mouth with light, sensuous kisses that made her blood boil.

"You are perfect. I love you, and words will never fully hold what's in my heart, but if you let me, sweetheart, I intend to show you, prove it to you. Every second of the day for the rest of my life. Permission to shoot me if I fail."

Her breath caught at the tenderness in his tone as she imagined the years ahead, his hands caressing her skin, hot words whispered in her ear. "Such a drama queen." She smiled as they swayed to their rhythm. "Magic," she sighed. "Sounds perfect, Winter. Now, show me your moves."

AUTHOR'S NOTE

Thank you for reading *KING'S CATCH* Book One in the Sentinel Security N.Y.C. series and I hope you enjoyed getting to know Winter and Maggie as much as I did.

Book Two in the series will out there later this year. Haven't decided if it will be Trigger or Storm who meets their match.

For those of you wondering if Spook and Crystal from the Sentinel Security London series get their HEA. Coming Soon.

If you are new to my heroes, you can read the Brit's stories:

Faithful

Saviour

Justice

If you want a fantastic bargain then read my story RUSH, along with sixteen other sizzling romances in the Guarded Hearts Protector Romance anthology.

Watch out for my novella in the BIG BAD AND RICH ANTHOLOGY due for release in November 2023. Pre-Order in May.

To keep up to date with all my news, excerpts, and free stuff, sign up for my newsletter at www.elizarenton.com

Or find me on Facebook https://www.facebook.com/elizarenton and Instagram https://www.instagram.com/elizarentonauthor

You can follow me on BookBub https://www.bookbub.com/authors/eliza-renton

How can you help authors if you liked their books? Tell your friends and family. Consider leaving a review at your favorite online book retailer.

Happy reading!

Eliza

ABOUT ELIZA RENTON

LOVE TAKES COURAGE

Eliza Renton writes Romantic Suspense featuring alpha protectors and strong women. She is a card-carry rain lover who enjoys walking, gardening, and eating ice cream in the rain. When she is not deep in the editing cave or listening to her characters, she hangs out with her knitting group or binge-watches action-packed films and TV.

Eliza thinks the best part of being a writer is visiting make-believe worlds and falling in love while others stress about parking spaces, their boss, and the cost of a cup of coffee.

www.ingramcontent.com/pod-product-compliance
Lightning Source LLC
Chambersburg PA
CBHW020511120726
47904CB00003B/788